Gabriel FALLEN

Empire Nightclub #2

K.A.TUCKER

Editing by Hot Tree Editing

Cover design by Shanoff Designs

Published by K.A. Tucker

GABRIEL FALLEN

From internationally bestselling author K.A. Tucker comes the dark and sexy Empire Nightclub series.

Mercy Wheeler and Gabriel Easton's sordid tale continues in Gabriel Fallen *as Mercy heads down a dangerous path.*

Gabriel has made an art of dangling what I'm most desperate for in front of me, what he knows I can't refuse, no matter the cost. In this case, that cost continues to be *me.*

He is still a scoundrel, but I'm beginning to see something more.

And while our bargain is proving advantageous in ways I never expected, the risks that come with being associated with a man like him are becoming painfully clear.

But how much longer before this arrangement with Gabriel costs me everything I am?

This is the second book in the Empire Nightclub series and should be read after Sweet Mercy

ONE
MERCY

Gabriel is my father's only hope.

This is my first thought as I crack my eyes at 5:55 a.m. It's the second day in a row that I've woken before my alarm.

And the third night that I've shared a bed with Gabriel Easton, son to the infamous Phoenix crime boss, Vlad Easton, a reality that still hasn't quite sunk in.

I spend a moment studying the sleeping man beside me. He's as beautiful unconscious as he is when his piercing dark blue eyes are sizing me up. It's a different kind of beautiful though. His chiseled features are relaxed, his thick fringe of long lashes grazing his cheeks, his pink pouty lips parted slightly. He looks almost boyish.

My gaze skates over his hard, muscular body, stomach-down, sinewy arms tucked beneath his pillow, the sheet draped provocatively over his hips. There is nothing boyish about that body, or how he used it last night to bring me pleasure I can still feel between my thighs.

Gabriel left me in the shower to stew over his wild proposition and wasn't in the bedroom when I emerged.

Instead of going looking for him—I wasn't in the mood to face his brother and the Pervert Posse, especially after the sordid little fuckfest I'd just so wantonly given in to—I replaced the soaked bedding with fresh sheets from the hallway closet, and then hunkered down with my textbooks to work on my school assignment.

It was to no avail though. I couldn't focus on anything but Gabriel's offer to hire a decent lawyer to appeal my father's murder conviction. I couldn't help but wonder if maybe a *really* good lawyer—the kind that Gabriel can no doubt afford—might get my father exonerated. At the very least, they could get a retrial and the charges reduced to involuntary manslaughter. Maybe also get him out of that hellhole, Fulcort Prison, in exchange for some place where he's not going to end up in a pine box six feet under.

All it will cost me is my dignity: selling my body to Gabriel for longer than the originally agreed upon week in exchange for him protecting my father in prison. I don't even know exactly what Gabriel has put into motion to protect my father from Fleet's cousin's wrath and whether it'll stick. Yet here I am, about to jump into bed with him—literally—for another offer.

How easy would it be to say yes to this proposition, and not only because it's a means to an end for this nightmare my father is living? If I'm being honest with myself, the last twenty-four hours have been a whirlwind but far from terrible. Lying in bed next to him now, remembering last night—the feel of his soft lips on my neck, his firm hands pinning mine above my head, his impressive length thrusting into me—has me clenching my thighs together in anticipation of a repeat.

Gabriel Easton is far different from the man I pegged him for.

But I can't forget who this man is. *What* he is. The son of a crime boss, a man who enjoys all the spoils that come with a life of corruption—of preying on the weak and vulnerable, of illicit affairs and lingering in the shadows, of countless money-making schemes that I couldn't conjure up if I tried, no doubt.

He says that's not who he is. I asked him point-blank if he was involved in dealing drugs, and he said no. I still don't know if I can believe him. I *want* to believe him.

Maybe I should for my own sake. Maybe in this shitty hand that life has dealt me, I need to learn how to accept the few advantages I've been offered, even if they're delivered with fingers as filthy as Gabriel's likely are.

I sigh. These were the thoughts that kept my mind swirling until I drifted off last night, and I know they'll dominate much of my day today.

The alarm on my phone fills the silent room. I rush to shut it off.

A soft groan sounds next to me, and I hold my breath, watching Gabriel as he stirs, slowly rolling onto his back. His thick throat works over a swallow; one arm slides to settle over his chiseled abdomen. But his eyes remain shut, his broad chest rising and falling in a rhythm.

The sheet does nothing to hide the impressive ridge between his legs where his morning erection awaits attention. Heat pools in my core as I imagine slipping my hand beneath the soft, white cotton to feel the velvety smooth skin against my palm, to wrap my fist around that firm, hot length and begin stroking.

He'd surely wake up then.

And I'm guessing I'd end up late for work.

Marsha is a stickler for her staff being on time.

Shrugging off the urge, I slip from bed and test the cold

tile against my bare feet. The tidy stack of books on my nightstand makes me pause. Gabriel must have collected them after I fell asleep. I don't know why that surprises me —that Gabriel would be considerate or thoughtful, that he would take the time to line them up neatly. He's already proven that he can be considerate, especially after that whole Ambien mess when he made the effort to meet me at work to explain what happened. Then he proceeded to fuck me on a table but *before* that, he was sweet.

Grabbing the outfit I laid out for today, I tiptoe to the bathroom and quickly get ready for my day. Then, stealing one last, longing glance at the sleeping man who has become equal parts captor and savior, I duck out.

A RASPY COUGH warns me of Caleb's presence in the kitchen before I round the corner. I stifle my groan and steel my nerve, preparing myself for another eyeful of man-whore penis. Something tells me Caleb enjoys shocking people by going full nude first thing in the morning. That or he's just that lazy. Either way, I'm not giving him the satisfaction of shocking me this time around.

I lock my gaze on the coffee maker, catching nothing more than his broad bare chest in my peripheral vision as I pass. "Good morning."

I get a grunt in response.

"Rough night?" I ask mildly, thinking about the tittering brunettes here when I got home from class. I fish another travel mug from the cupboard, reminding myself to bring in yesterday's from the car when I get home tonight so I don't begin a collection.

Not home.

Here.

To Gabriel's.

"Well, I can usually just sit back and let Rhonda ride my dick all night, minimal work. But Mindy or Misty or whatever the fuck her name is takes some real hip action and a thumb in her ass to—"

"A 'yes' would have sufficed," I cut him off sharply, focusing on the buttons on the machine, my cheeks burning. "Sounds like you should be sleeping still."

"I don't sleep much. You know, insomnia or some shit."

"That sucks." One would think Caleb should be perpetually exhausted, given his active sex life.

"It does. How was *your* night?"

"Fine." I'm not used to talking to anyone this early. I'm not used to being awake this early either. If I were at my apartment in downtown Phoenix, only a ten-minute drive from the drug addiction center where I work, I'd still be asleep for another hour.

"Hmm. From what Gabe told me, you should still be sleeping, too." I hear the laughter in Caleb's tone.

My jaw clenches. That Gabriel might have given his brother illicit details about last night bothers me for some reason. The way he looked down at me, the way his fingers stroked my jaw, it all felt intimate and private.

The sputtering of coffee spitting into my cup is the only sound in the kitchen for a long moment, and I relish the momentary break in obscene conversation with Gabriel's older brother.

Caleb wordlessly sets the carton of cream on the counter next to me.

"Thank you." I reach for a spoon, feeling his steady, assessing gaze on me.

"Of course, he kept some in the tank for later, when he

showed up to my room and took Misty off my hands. Thank fucking God because—"

"What?" I hiss, my stomach dropping with the clatter of the spoon against the counter. My eyes flash to Caleb, noting absently the boxer briefs he's wearing this time. "Gabriel was with one of those women last night?" It comes out in a whisper. He was fucking another woman after he just finished fucking *and* propositioning me?

Rage and hurt flare inside me.

Caleb's eyes narrow as he studies me closely. "Nah, I'm only kidding."

I match his gaze and try to decipher if he's lying now or if he was lying before.

He nods, as if deciding something. "Yeah ... I thought so."

"You thought so, what?"

He takes a long sip of orange juice, his jutting Adam's apple bobbing with each swallow. Caleb is an attractive man—almost as attractive as Gabriel—with a perfect, muscular physique and a handsome face. He's also rich. It's not a wonder that he has women tripping over themselves to get to him. The ones who don't know or don't care what he may have done, that is.

Glass emptied, he sets it down on the quartz countertop with a clank. "You're as into my idiot brother as he is into you."

"Your idiot brother is treating me like a prostitute," I throw back. Meanwhile my mind is working overtime. *Gabriel's into me?* What does that even mean? What *exactly* did Gabriel tell Caleb last night?

"If that's the case, you are one expensive piece of ass." Caleb saunters toward the front door and punches in the alarm code. "Gabe's not one for getting up in the morning. I guess if you're going to be staying here awhile, we better get you set up with your own code to this door so you're not trapped on the off chance that I'm actually asleep at this hour."

I take that as my cue to leave, which I'm more than happy to do. Dumping a touch more cream into my coffee, I collect my things and head for the door, trying not to stare too hard at Caleb's cut back. Thank God his proclivity to fuck anything that moves ensures I don't feel a shred of desire for him. If he were less of an obvious whore, I have a feeling the dynamics under this roof might be different.

His hand sits on the handle, his nails bitten down to the quick.

"Have a great day doing *whatever* it is you occupy your time doing," I offer, waiting for him to open the door. Maybe it's Caleb who gets his hands dirty in the family business. Maybe he's the one running the show now that their father is behind bars. I really have no idea about this man, beyond what Caleb sounds like when he orgasms.

Caleb sighs, shakes his head. "Do me a favor and don't dick my brother around."

I can't help it, I snort. "I think Gabriel is the one doing the dicking, and he's quite happy about it."

But Caleb doesn't find my joke funny, a scowl forming over his handsome features. "He's eager to put himself in the crosshairs and it's for you."

That gives me pause. "What does that mean?"

"Exactly what it sounds like." Caleb eases the front door, resting his muscular forearm against its edge, his handsome face cast in a rare serious expression. "I don't think my little brother appreciates how dangerous the shitstorm he's about to pull us into is."

"A shitstorm for what? Hiring a lawyer for my father?" What's dangerous about that?

Caleb chuckles in a way that tells me I have no idea what's going on. "For becoming someone else." He steps back and winks at me. "Have a wonderful day helping drug addicts with their vices." At least this time, he doesn't call for my attention, instead shutting the heavy front door behind me after I march through.

It's quiet outside—not surprising, at this early hour. The cars in the driveway are gone, so whoever Caleb screwed didn't stay the night.

I head for my dented, dusty Toyota, replaying Caleb's words, his body language, trying to figure out what he meant about the danger. What danger could Gabriel be putting himself into for me? More danger than usual, given he's an Easton? And is it the kind of danger that puts him in Fulcort?

Or the kind that puts him in an unmarked hole in the desert?

Will Gabriel suddenly disappear from my life one day, never to be heard from again? An unexpected pang stirs in my chest at that thought.

With a heavy sigh, I sink into my driver seat and crank the engine. It sputters and coughs but won't turn. "No ..." I try again, and it's the same thing. This isn't surprising, but it's not like I can hop on a bus, being all the way up here. "Come on, come on, come on," I coax, holding the key in place, listening to my car choke, hoping something inside will catch.

But eventually all I get for my effort is a clicking sound, which is far less promising than the choking.

"Shit!" I slam my hands on the steering wheel in frustration, wondering how I'm going to get into work now.

That's when one of the garage doors begins slowly rolling open. Behind it is the SUV Gabriel drove to meet me yesterday for lunch and a bleary-eyed Gabriel, his hair wild from bed, wearing nothing but a pair of loose sweatpants. They hang low on his hips, showing off his beautiful, bare torso, the thick pad of muscles over his abdomen, the deep V cut of his hips.

And the distinguishable bulge farther below.

The entire sight steals several beats of my heart.

"Won't start?" he asks in a raspy morning voice, reaching up to hook his hands on the underside of the garage door, stretching his body, making his pants sink lower.

My blood stirs in anticipation of them sliding right off. Hell, I *want* them to drop right to the cold, dirty pavement. I want to watch him reach down and begin stroking himself like he did last night.

When did I turn into such a pervert?

Gabriel smirks as if he can read my thoughts.

Where did you go after our shower though?

Did he fuck that brunette in Caleb's room? Did he go and have some super weird, super dirty orgy? Is that where he was after being with me?

Those questions effectively douse the early morning flames that burn bright for the man in front of me. The only danger around here is Gabriel, I decide, easing out of my dead car. "No." I don't have the energy for a wittier answer.

"Sounds like the alternator."

"I wouldn't know." My dad would, but he's lying in an infirmary bed in prison at the moment. I sigh. "I'll call Billy and have him come with the tow truck as soon as he can."

"That thing shouldn't be on the road."

"I agree, but if I'm going to be all the way out here,

where people haven't ever heard of public transit," I make a point of sounding put out, "then that thing has to get me to work."

Backing up toward the SUV, Gabriel fishes out a set of keys from his pocket. "Take the Lincoln. I was going to tell you to take it this morning anyway, if you hadn't snuck out of bed." His tone is accusatory.

I eye the luxury vehicle. "I can't," I mumble, half-heartedly. Why can't I? At least it's not the Lambo. *That*, I definitely can't show up to an addiction center in. Besides, I have no desire to get behind that wheel. God forbid, I'd trade paint with someone and be indebted to Gabriel for life.

But I need a car. The luxury SUV is a car.

I should take it.

I should take it and park at the hair salon one block down, so no one at work sees me driving up in it. I can't answer those questions.

"Come on ... you know you want to." Gabriel jangles the keys, tempting me as my conscience battles it out. "And it's the only way you're getting in to work today."

I sigh, collect my bags from my Toyota, and slam my door shut. As if I have a choice here.

I saunter toward him, his dark gaze drifting over my emerald green sundress down to my bare legs, a hungry gleam in them. Much like the one he had last night from the moment he came around that corner in swim shorts to the moment he left the shower. The way he always seems to be looking at me.

My stomach tightens as I'm hit with another mental flash from last night, this one of him positioned over me in bed, his body tense as he thrusts into me. But it's immediately followed by one of him with that Misty-Minnie-Mary-whoever-the-fuck, and my stomach twists.

"Were you with your brother and his friends last night?" I blurt out.

Gabriel blinks, then frowns, seemingly caught off guard. "What do you mean by 'with'?"

"Did you fuck another woman last night?" I can't hide the accusation in my tone. If he did screw one of them, I'll be upset, and that notion angers me. I *don't want* to care who Gabriel's with, but I'm quickly realizing that I do. Our relationship—or whatever I should call it—changed yesterday. Somewhere between the soft kisses and the gentle strokes and the unguarded words, something between us changed.

He chuckles, and that only infuriates me more. "No. I didn't touch anyone else last night. I had to talk to my brother." A curious look casts over his face. "Why are you asking?"

I study his eyes another long moment. I can't see a lie in them. But would I be able to? Stupid Caleb. I sigh and hold out my hand to accept the keys. "Thank you."

His pouty lips twist into a sly smile. "You're welcome. Let me show you a few things on it." He leads me around to the driver side, his bare feet—damn it, even his feet are sexy—padding over the concrete floor. Opening the door, he leans against it and points out several buttons. "If you want to use the nav system ..." I can't help tuning him out, my focus more on the cut of his arms and his flat nipples and how I can make out the outline of the tip of his penis in his sweatpants.

"Mercy? Did you hear me?"

I swallow against the sudden dryness in my mouth. "It's a car, not a rocket. I'll figure it out."

"Is something the matter?" he asks lightly, like he knows why I'm so distracted. He's so damn erotic looking right now, with his messy bedhead and his sleepy eyes.

"No reason. Thanks for lending me this. I'll make sure to return it without a scratch." I toss my things across to the passenger side and then climb into the leather seat that Gabriel occupied yesterday, sliding my palms over the steering wheel. Definitely an upgrade from my Toyota.

"I wasn't with another woman last night, Mercy," he says suddenly, in a more conciliatory tone, his steady gaze on mine, weighing me down. "I have no interest in touching anyone but you."

"Okay. That's ..." I swallow, peering into his eyes, seeing the truth in them. "Okay."

"So, do you have an answer for me?" He reaches up to rest his arms atop the SUV, giving me another sublime view of his body and the jutting cock that seems to be the only thing holding his sweatpants up at the moment.

He's *very* hard.

I peel my eyes away from his body to meet his stormy blue eyes.

Yes.

Yes, I'll stay here. Yes, I'll fuck Gabriel for the foreseeable future to get what I want and something I was so sure I didn't want.

It's on the tip of my tongue, but I bite it back and ask instead, "About what?"

His lips curl. "You're too smart to play dumb, Mercy. About my offer. The new deal."

A deal. That's what this is. And yet, the way he looks at me, the way he seems to care for me—whether I've eaten, whether I've slept, that I'm in a safe car—I could be legitimately dumb enough to fool myself into thinking he's a boyfriend. But I'm not. I'm more like his property, I remind myself. He's just protecting his investment.

I settle on, "I need more time." Not to decide what my answer is, but to figure out how I'm going to reconcile my pride in order to give it.

Gabriel's chest rises with a deep breath. "Okay," he says simply.

I feel my eyebrow arch. "Okay?" I was expecting more of a fight.

"I'm not going to force you to do anything you don't want to do."

I laugh, but it sounds hollow. *No. You're just going to dangle a golden carrot within easy reach.*

His bottom lip slides between his teeth, drawing my gaze to it. "But I think maybe you need help deciding."

"What do you—Ah!" I squeal as his warm hand grips my bare thigh. He swings my body around to face him, leaving my legs to dangle over the side. In seconds they're hoisted up against his shoulders, forcing me back until my head rests on the center console.

He wastes no time hiking my dress up and pulling down my panties.

"Gabriel!" I hiss, struggling to squirm out of his grip even as my blood races south. Warm morning air kisses my sensitive flesh. "I have to get to work!"

"Nice try. You don't start until eight." His gaze is alight with fire as it shifts from my eyes down to the apex of my legs. "And from what I can see, you won't last long." He runs a fingertip through my slit, eliciting a soft gasp from my lips.

"But we're in the garage. The cameras—"

"Are not in here," he assures, his palms hinting affection as they slide the length of my legs in a caressing manner to guide my panties the rest of the way off. He tosses them onto the dash before reaching down to push my thighs farther apart.

Whatever inclination I had to tell Gabriel to stop has faded from existence as I watch him drop to his knees on the hard concrete, his face at the perfect level.

"You're beautiful. Did you know that?" His fingertips prod, exposing everything that's private and hidden. "So tight, so pink, so ..." His mouth closes over me.

I sigh with the feel of the first long swipe of his tongue along my seam, a whisper of "oh my God," escaping me with his teasing swirl, his stubbled face scraping deliciously against my sensitive skin. The apprehension I felt over being bare like this, out in the garage, quickly evaporates, too rapt with Gabriel's undivided attention to getting me off. His powerful shoulders hold the weight of my calves, his eyes hooded as he licks and sucks and kisses my sex with the same intensity he had for my mouth last night.

My head propped against the console gives me a sublime view from this angle. Behind Gabriel the Lambo sits low to the ground, with just enough light coming from outside and with just the right angle from its low position to cast a reflection of the sordid scene. It's the most erotic thing I've ever seen, and my body is quickening in response.

Gabriel moans. The vibration courses deep through me, and heat floods my core; a tingle dances along my spine.

He smiles, pulling back just enough to let me watch the tip of his tongue slide through me. "You like my mouth on you, don't you?"

I hum my agreement.

"What about this? You like this, too?" He pushes two fingers into my slick entrance, followed by a third that stretches me wide. He begins pumping in and out, stroking a sensitive spot deep inside me with each pass, all while using his thumb on my swollen clit. With each stroke, more moisture builds in my core. The sound of my body's response to him should be embarrassing, but I find myself pushing my pelvis forward, desperate to give him more access—if that's even possible.

He watches me gyrate with concentrated interest. "You ready, babe?"

"Yes," I whisper breathlessly, reaching forward to weave my fingertips through his soft, boyish hair, free of whatever product he styles it with thanks to the epic shower session last night. There's no biting my tongue anymore, my voice dripping with desperation.

Slipping his fingers from my body, he stands and shucks his sweatpants, leaving me to admire his perfect, naked body. Leaning over me, he reaches into a small compartment beneath the navigation screen to pull out a condom.

"Someone's prepared," I mutter, though there's no animosity in my tone.

"Put it there yesterday, just for you." His eyes twinkle as he catches the edge of the foil wrapper between his teeth and tears it open.

"Right." I laugh at the bold lie.

His focus is momentarily on himself as he rolls the condom over his swollen tip and down, and I admire the hard planes of chiseled muscle. With that ready, whatever patience and leisure he showed when going down on me is gone, replaced by a man on a furtive mission.

He sinks into me with a single, hard thrust.

I cry out at the sudden invasion and the overwhelming sensation of being stretched by his impressive size.

Gabriel guides my legs back up to rest my ankles atop his shoulders, pressing his lips against one of them. "Need a minute to get used to me?" he whispers, trailing the tip of his tongue over my skin.

Physically, yes.

Mentally ...

Jesus. I should be on my way to work. How on earth did *this* happen? Oh, that's right. Gabriel showed up.

That's all he seems to have to do, and bam! I'm naked.

"I like this color on you." He reaches for the straps of the emerald green dress I chose for work and pushes them off my shoulders, allowing enough give to work the front down over my strapless bra. "Take it off. I want to see your tits move when I fuck you."

His filthy words hit me right where we're joined, and my body pulses with need.

It's too difficult to fuss with the clasp so I force the black lace garment down to settle where the rest of my dress is bunched on my rib cage.

Gabriel groans and takes one of my breasts in his palm, his thumb lazily stroking over my budded nipple. "I'm going to suck on these for hours tonight," he promises. Kicking his sweatpants off his left leg, he drags my body farther out until my hips are off the edge of the seat. Repositioning himself with one foot on the floor of the driver side, he braces himself.

And then his hips start moving.

It's all I can do to muffle my cries of pleasure as Gabriel slams into my body in a punishing rhythm, his fingertips digging into my thighs, his beautiful, muscular body straining with tension, his eyes searing as they move from where he's impaling me to my jolting breasts, to my face.

With each thrust, he sinks deep, his expert angle ensuring he hits the mark. In minutes, I feel the building pressure at the base of my spine. I no longer care that we're in his garage, that the door is open, that sound probably carries well into the calm morning and the everyone on the mountain knows one of the Easton brothers is having sex.

I don't hide from Gabriel how much I'm enjoying this, my lips falling open as my cries grow louder. Raw pleasure floods my pelvis and thighs and belly. I reach down between us to touch myself and draw it out, my inner muscles tightening, contracting around Gabriel's length as wave after wave of intense pleasure hits me.

An almost pained expression twists his face. With five quick, hard thrusts, it happens—his cock swells and his hips still and I feel him pulsating deep inside me. The primal moan that escapes his lips boasts immense satisfaction.

I stare up at his naked, glistening chest as it heaves, and I imagine for a moment that there is no barrier between us, that he's spilling his seed deep inside me.

My inner muscles clamp over his cock with the illicit thought.

A panting, spent Gabriel leans forward, resting his forehead on the Lincoln's doorframe while he catches his breath, swallowing several times, his sexy throat bobbing. "Jesus, I can't last with you." He smooths his palms up and down over my thighs as if to soothe where he gripped them so tightly. "I'm sorry if I was a bit rough. I got carried away."

It's okay, I want to say, but I can't seem to find my tongue, my body a limp rag. If he weren't holding my legs up, they'd be splayed and useless, hanging out the door.

"Yo, Gabe! Since you're up, let's hit the green at eight?"

I startle at the sound of Caleb's booming voice from somewhere unseen, instantly tensing up. I try to pull away, but Gabriel holds me in place, still inside me, and shifts his hips to block the view from the back of the garage, where I'm guessing the door to the house is. "Yeah, fine, whatever."

"Weren't you supposed to leave for work a while ago, Mercy?" Caleb calls, and I hear the laughter in his voice.

I close my eyes in mortification, my cheeks flushing.

"Come on! Get the fuck outta here," Gabriel growls, but his eyes remain on my face.

"Yeah, yeah. It's not like it's a big deal. I've seen it all before, a thousand times." The heavy steel door shuts a moment later, leaving us in awkward silence, the reality that we're basically outside—the garage door is wide open—sinking in again.

"How long was he watching for?" I dare ask, dreading the answer.

"I don't know, but don't worry. He wouldn't have seen much from there," Gabriel promises, easing out of me. He peels the filled condom off and tosses it somewhere unseen, and then reaches for my discarded panties. He slips them over first one foot, then the other, ever so gingerly, and slides them up into place. His brow furrows when they cover me up, almost as if he's disappointed to have my most private part hidden from his view.

Gripping me by the waist, Gabriel hoists me to a sitting position and then quietly watches as I adjust my bra and slip my straps back over my shoulders.

With a delicate touch, he guides my legs back to the proper position for driving and feeds the seat belt around my chest, securing it in the clasp. His heated eyes are locked on mine as he adjusts my seat. "Press the brake."

I follow instructions without thinking, and he hits the ignition button. The engine comes to life with a soft purr.

"You good?" he asks, leaning in to lay teasing kisses against my jaw, his stubble scratching against my skin.

I shiver. "I'm fine." In truth, my brain is a little foggy.

That he's being so sweet and caring doesn't help. That he's still standing naked beside me *definitely* doesn't help.

"So, do you have a different answer for me now?" His voice is soft and husky.

I close my eyes, reveling in the intoxicating feel of his plush, skilled mouth on me. "I guess it depends on how good this lawyer is." I pause. "And, like I said before, I have terms."

"Terms ..." His fingertip settles on my chin, steering my face to his. Amusement flickers in his eyes. "What terms?"

"I'll let you know when I decide on them." I hate that I sound breathless.

"Hmm." His long lashes flutter as his gaze drops to my lips. "Maybe I should come up with a few of my own then."

"Go ahead. We can negotiate." I steel my nerve and drop my gaze to his lower half, to his still-hard length, and echo his earlier words. "Though something tells me you won't last too long."

His answering chuckle vibrates down to my core. He plants a slow but sizzling kiss on my mouth, letting me taste myself on him, sucking hard once on my bottom lip before finally pulling back. "Drive safe and call me later. 'Kay, baby?"

I nod mutely, checking the clock on the dash. I still have plenty of time to get in, which is good because I'm feeling discombobulated. I'll need to drive extra slow this morning.

He backs away, reaching down to pick his track pants off the cement floor. They dangle from his fingertips. He makes no effort to redress, allowing me ample opportunity to admire his nakedness.

I must still be in a daze because I can't seem to stop from staring.

"Why don't you just call in sick?" he suggests, smirking.

If I don't get out of here right now, I'm liable to do just that and then beg him to take me back to bed.

Snapping out of my lustful stupor, I press on the gas pedal. The tires squeal as the SUV lurches forward with far more power than I expect. After adjusting the pressure on the pedal, I coast down the driveway.

A glance in my rearview mirror finds Gabriel standing in the center of the now empty space, looking delectable as he watches me leave, unashamed of his nakedness.

A deep ache stirs between my thighs.

"I am so fucked," I mutter, shaking my head.

TWO
GABRIEL

"Should I call someone to tow that hunk of shit out of here?" Caleb's focus is on his bowl of cereal when I reenter the kitchen. "Neighbors are going to complain. I think there's a community ordinance against using our property as a scrap yard."

"There's probably also one for having orgies in your backyard, but like you give a fuck about the neighbors anyway." I fish out a coffee mug and brew myself a cup. It's early—way too early for my sorry ass—but there's no way I'm going back to sleep now, with Mercy's taste all over my mouth. I can't wait until I have her all over my dick. Which reminds me, I need to go in for blood work today.

I feel my brother's eyes on my back.

"So, did she manage to screw the insanity out of you?"

I smirk. "On the contrary, I think she just made me more insane." I woke up to find the bed beside me empty again, but the smell of her rosewater body shit still lingered in the bathroom, telling me I hadn't missed her by that long.

That had me running.

Fucking *running* for a woman. When have I ever done that?

I could hear her car from inside, choking and sputtering as Mercy tried to start it in vain. I'm not gonna lie, I'm pretty happy the Toyota died. It was like providence. God telling me not to waste another minute and fuck her in the Lincoln. It was all I could do not to tear her panties right off her perfect hips.

Jesus. I'm rock-hard again, just thinking about the sound of her cries.

Does she have any idea what she does to me? Here she is, coming up with her "terms." Little does she know, she could demand I wear a goddamn ball gag every day of the week and I might agree, as long as I'm doing it while my dick is buried inside her.

She was *so* wet for me today. Though, she always is. She can pretend to hate me all she wants, but that secret spot tells no lies.

"So, what are we gonna do?" Caleb asks around a mouthful of food. "You want to set up a meeting with the Perris or should I?"

I pinch the bridge of my nose against the threatening headache that comes with that prospect. Caleb and I spent hours in the cellar last night, pacing in circles, strategizing a game plan for how to approach Merrick and Vince Perri now that they've made contact. Aside from finding out *exactly* what those two have in mind in their bid to disconnect themselves from their family's drug business, we haven't come up with anything concrete. "No, I'll do it. Your temper is liable to get in the way." There's a reason they came to me in the first place—I'm the levelheaded one. "Give me some time to think about it."

"We need to be careful," Caleb warns. "For all we

know, this is a trap. Plus, if anyone catches wind of this, they'll start asking questions." By anyone, he means Uncle Peter, who has his own network of eyes and ears everywhere. For a guy who preaches respect and loyalty, he's a sneaky fuck. Then again, our father has his own web of eyes and ears trained on the goings-on of Uncle Peter and our cousins. Hell, on us, too.

"Yup," I mumble dismissively, pulling out my phone. "I've got to call DeHavilland."

"DeHavilland? Really? You're pulling out the big guns for her?" My brother gives me a questioning look. "That guy's going to rake you over the coals."

"I'd expect nothing less." Justin DeHavilland is the best lawyer in the state. He's also one of the most expensive sons-of-bitches out there. He's made a killing off our family, but he's also earned his money. With a less skilled defense, my dad would be away for the rest of his life on conspiracy to commit murder at the very least. Mercy's father got hosed with his tool of a lawyer and a vindictive prosecutor with something to prove. If anyone can sort out the shoddy mess he got buried under, it's Justin.

And the sooner Mercy sees that I'm not playing around here, the sooner she'll stop pretending she doesn't want a repeat of this morning ... every day. That woman wants me as much as I want her, whether she'll admit it or not.

But I want her to fucking admit it.

Hell, I *need* her to admit it.

"It's 6:45 a.m.," Caleb reminds me as I search my speed dial.

"With the kind of retainer we pay, we can call him at 3:45 a.m. Besides, he's up."

And if he's not, he's damn well going to be.

THREE
MERCY

It's a quarter after eleven when my desk phone rings. It's Ali from Reception.

"There's a man here to see you," she says.

"Gabriel?" My heart begins racing with excitement. Would he show up at my work again?

"No, not him. A different man." She drops her voice to a whisper. "Older. And rich-looking."

I frown. Who else besides Gabriel would be showing up at Mary's to see me? "Did he say who he is?" I ask warily.

"I think he said he was a lawyer?" I can just imagine our bubbly receptionist covering the receiver with her hand, her bright blue eyes sizing him up. "He said he's here to talk to you about your dad's appeal."

"My dad's a-appeal," I stammer, staring at the sad budget spreadsheet on my computer monitor, though none of the numbers are registering anymore. But that would mean Gabriel has already hired a lawyer, though I haven't agreed to anything yet. So either he's sure I will agree or he wants to make sure that I take his deal.

My chest swells at the fervor with which he seems to be

chasing me, even if his intentions are entirely scandalous. Though, he was so sweet to me this morning. I assumed he told me to text him when I got to work because that's just what you say to the woman you drove your dick into mercilessly, but he texted me at 8:02 to make sure I'd made it fine.

If I didn't know better, I'd say he's acting like a caring boyfriend.

But boyfriend material, Gabriel is not.

"I'll be there in a sec." I hang up the phone. Smoothing the creases out of my dress that I earned thanks to Gabriel, I rush for the front lobby.

Ali nods toward a man in a gray pinstriped suit. It's unnecessary, given he's the only man there and he's pacing the length of the narrow waiting room, a phone pressed to his ear. Even before he turns around, I know this lawyer isn't from the same planet as the one we hired. That guy looked like he shopped for his suits at the thrift store and his brown hair was perpetually unkempt. This guy's suit is custom-tailored, sleek on his fit body, and his mane of silver hair is thick and styled, not a stray hair out of place.

He turns around and, upon seeing me, does the briefest of once-overs before mumbling something into his phone and hanging up. "Miss Wheeler?" Even his voice sounds rich.

"Yes. That's me."

He strolls forward purposefully and introduces himself with a firm handshake and a tight-lipped smile. If he's bothered by meeting a potential client in a drug rehab center, he doesn't let on.

He's an attractive, clean-shaven older man of about sixty, with shrewd, hazel-green eyes and a strong nose. He smells luxurious, too—unlike shyster lawyer's choking aftershave. "My name's Justin DeHavilland. Mr. Easton hired me to help with your father's case. Is there somewhere private that we can talk?"

"Um ..." I look to Ali, whose attention is rapt. People like this do not step foot inside Mary's.

She quickly scans the meeting room schedule, but cringes. "Room Three is free but only for the next ten minutes—"

"That'll be fine. This is just a brief touch base. Please, Miss Wheeler." Justin holds a manicured hand out, and I catch a glimpse of the pricey gold watch, the tiny diamonds at the hour marks winking at me.

I lead him into the farthest of our small meeting rooms, used for private counseling sessions. None of the rooms are particularly comfortable—with hard chairs and yellow walls meant to inspire a sunny and bright mood but instead they just look washed out and dank—but this one seems especially rough. There's a hole in the drywall where a frustrated client punched it and a bucket in the corner to catch water from the leak in our roof, now that we're in monsoon season.

By the flat gaze Justin offers the room before sitting down, I'd say he notices the sad state of our building. It's almost comical to see him in here. My guess is, if I added the cost of his suit and his watch together, I'd be well into five digits.

"Gabriel Easton has asked me to represent your father in an appeal on his murder conviction," he says, jumping right in. "I assume you have copies of his court documents? Of course I can request them through the courts, but this would be faster."

"At home. Yeah."

"Okay. If you could bring them all down to me at my office. Here's the address." He slides a business card across the table. "Who represented your father for the original case?"

"Melvin Burns."

Justin's brow furrows. "Who?"

"Exactly." I don't care to waste my ten minutes talking about that idiot. "Do you really think you can help my father? Can you get him out of there?" There's no mistaking the hopefulness in my voice.

He gives me a one-sided shrug. "Gabriel gave me a brief rundown of his situation. I need a lot more information, but based on what I've heard, I'd say we have a strong case for an appeal. And if not ... I'll find a case for an appeal."

I swallow my nerves, not wanting to get too excited. "And how long will an appeal take?"

"One to two years at best, a lot longer at worst." Another one of those noncommittal shrugs. "Having connections with the law clerks can help speed things up."

"And do you? Have connections with the clerks?"

He waits a beat and then flashes a perfect row of capped, white teeth. "I have connections everywhere, darling."

"That's good." It hasn't escaped me that it's not even noon and this fancy, rich lawyer came down to Mary's to introduce himself to me. He likely dropped whatever he had planned for the morning to do so. I doubt this is normal protocol for a high-end lawyer.

Gabriel must be an important client of his.

I hesitate. "Do you normally represent Gabriel's affairs?"

"My firm is retained by the Easton family for their legal needs," he answers smoothly. A practiced response.

What about for their illegal needs?

He said the Easton family. That encompasses more than just Gabriel. "So, like, Gabriel's father, too?"

He blinks. "Right."

My blood begins to pump harder through my veins as I put two and two together. Oh my God. I have a crime family's lawyer helping my father get out of prison.

I note that there's no discussion of if Justin is representing my father, no question of if I'm accepting Gabriel's deal. Not that Justin has any clue about any deal, I'm sure. He doesn't want to know his client's sordid personal affairs unless it pertains to a case. But Gabriel's already assuming that I have accepted, or he's making sure that I do by parading this fancy lawyer here in front of me.

Well played.

"I'll want to familiarize myself with the case before I go to Fulcort to meet with your father. Duncan Wheeler is his name, correct?"

"Yes." My father. "He was attacked by another prisoner about a week and a half ago. He spent some time in the hospital. I don't know when he'll be out of the infirmary. I can't get any information out of them."

"I'll call to find out and let you know. Either way, they have to allow me in to see him if I'm his lawyer."

I swallow hard. "Right, about that." How do I say this delicately? "Is there any way you could tell him that you're taking this case pro bono?"

Justin's eyes narrow.

"I mean, of course you're not," I quickly add. "But I just think it would be best if he doesn't ask too many questions. About anything." But especially about Gabriel and why on earth he'd be so willing to foot the bill. My dad may not be highly educated but he's not a stupid man. He'll figure out at least part of this situation—the part where I'm sleeping with the son of the convicted crime boss in the same prison as my father. If that happens, my dad will refuse Justin's legal help.

Justin's not a stupid man either. I can almost see the pieces clicking together in his brain. His lips twist. "My firm has been known to do pro bono. Once or twice."

"So this could be the third time, as far as my father knows then?" I dare ask. Is it even legal to hide the source of lawyer fees this way? Though something tells me the lawyer of a crime family knows how to obscure the line of what's legal to suit his clients just fine.

He holds his manicured hands out, palms up. "The Eastons pay me either way."

"That's especially the part I'd like him to not know about. The Eastons paying, I mean. He can't find that out, under any circumstances."

"Then he won't," Justin says simply.

Let out a shaky breath. "Okay."

"Sounds like we have"—he checks his watch—"six minutes for you to fill me in."

Am I agreeing to Gabriel's latest offer by continuing on with this? I guess I could renege. He can't do much without all the case file paperwork. I have his business card. I could call to tell him that I'm out, that he should bill Gabriel for his time and not make the drive out to Fulcort.

But I already know that I'm not going to do that.

Well played, indeed, Gabriel.

"You're his sex slave!" Michelle's bright eyes widen on the word sex.

"Shut up!" I glance around the coffee shop to make sure

no one heard her. Thankfully, most people are on their way home from work or meeting up for wine at local bars, something I would gladly have done tonight if I wasn't worried that one glass would turn to ten as a way of dealing with my current level of anxiety. "I haven't agreed to it yet."

She rolls her eyes. "You raced home over lunch to get your files so you could drop them off at the lawyer dude's office. Uh, yeah, you have."

"I just wanted to make sure Justin's firm wasn't in the back of some dodgy warehouse." That's not entirely a lie. A crime family's lawyer has to be shady as fuck. And maybe he is, but his firm takes up the top several floors of a downtown Phoenix glass skyscraper. Not only that, Justin is a named partner. DeHavilland, Arnold, and Gold.

His name is first, and not because it's alphabetical.

I left the files with the receptionist, who promised to get them to Justin as soon as he was back from his lunch meeting, and then I scurried back to Mary's to spend the afternoon pretending to work while I researched everything I could on the Easton crime family's lawyer, who is, from everything I found out on him, the very best of the best. As in, anyone caught with a smoking gun in their hand who can afford to go to him, goes to him. And it appears that no client of his ever goes down for what Prosecution has pegged them for. And some are outright acquitted.

As in, had my father had Justin defending him in the first place, he might not have ever seen a day inside Fulcort's cold, concrete walls.

Even Gabriel's father was found not guilty of half the crimes they tried to pin on him that, I'm guessing, he was guilty as sin of.

"And now that you know this lawyer is legit and awesome?" Michelle prods with a knowing smile.

"Now ... I guess we'll see how tonight goes." A shiver of anticipation courses through me. What will happen when I get home? Will Gabriel be waiting for me again like he was last night? Will he manage to seduce me five minutes after I've fooled myself into thinking I can resist him? I don't have time for another long, drawn-out shower fuck. I have assignments to finish for tomorrow night's class.

My best friend's eyes narrow before they widen. "Oh my God! Mercy! You're so into him!"

"No, I am so not!" I deny, just as my phone chirps with an incoming text. Lo and behold, it's from Gabriel. It's as if he has some sixth sense.

Gabriel: Rosita made another batch of carnitas. You on your way home yet?

Excitement stirs in my stomach. Home. He's waiting for me. All however many pounds of glorious, rippling, hard muscle and eight inches—at least—of pleasure are waiting for me.

I quickly text back:

Mercy: Having coffee with Michelle. Be back by seven.

As soon as I hit send, I regret it. I'm not his girlfriend, I remind myself. And I shouldn't answer to his beckoning.

I send a follow-up text:

Mercy: Or eight. I'll be back when I'm ready. And I'll be finishing an assignment and studying for my upcoming exams.

Michelle has to leave soon for an appointment so I will be home by seven, but there's no reason to make Gabriel think that I'm dropping everything and running to him, that he has the upper hand here. But maybe he expects that. Now that he's set up Justin, is he going to start demanding that I ask how high when he says jump?

Gabriel: The cute blond from Empire?

Mercy: Yes.

Gabriel: You should invite her over. I'm sure Caleb would love to meet her.

Mercy: Why would I do that to my best friend?

"What's that grin for?" Michelle asks, angling to catch a glimpse of my screen. "Are you talking about me?"

"No. Well, yes. Gabriel said you should come over and meet Caleb—"

"Okay!"

I fix her with a flat look. "No, Michelle."

"Is he as hot as his brother?"

"Some might think so." Though I'd disagree. No one's as attractive as Gabriel. "But, trust me, you don't want anything to do with him. See that knot in the wood over there?"

She follows my finger toward the side of the counter, where the owners have finished it off with pine. "Yeah?"

"He'd stick his dick in that."

She bursts out in laughter.

"I'm not kidding," I continue, but I'm laughing too. "He'd walk up there, whip down his pants—if he's even wearing any, because the guy walks around the house naked—and pop it right in, in front of everyone here."

"He's really that bad?"

"The guy has had several women over every night that I've been there. He fucked one of them on the patio in front of his friends."

Her button nose wrinkles.

"Exactly. You want nothing to do with that."

She chews her lip. "What about Gabriel?"

"What about him? You're not getting with him!" I rush to warn before I can catch myself.

Her eyebrows arch. "I was asking if you've seen him with anyone else, but wow, jealous much?"

"I'm not jealous," I deny, thinking back to his hands on that twiggy redhead. Is what he said to me this morning true? That he has no interest in anyone else? Or is that just a lie on top of the other lies he's told me? Is he just telling me what he knows I need to hear? "And, no. He's been too busy trying to hump my leg every spare minute."

We share a giggle.

"So, he's that good, huh?" Michelle ask, her eyes twinkling behind a sip of coffee.

I glance around to make sure no one's watching, and then shift in my seat and slide the bottom of my dress up to show her the small, dark bruises on my thighs. I noticed them while using the restroom earlier. "From his fingers, this morning."

She gasps. "Oh my God. Did he hurt you?"

"No, it definitely didn't hurt," I admit, relaying the scene from the garage, my cheeks flushing a touch. "He treats me well." Better than well. He treats me like something to be cherished and protected.

"Damn ..." She fans herself with a used napkin. "In that driver seat?" She nods to the SUV parked just outside. After a day of driving it, I don't know how I'm ever going to get back into my shitty Toyota.

I grin sheepishly.

"No offense, but I would already have ditched you and raced home if I had that waiting for me. Why are you still here?"

I sigh. "Because this all comes at a cost, Michelle. I haven't figured out what I'm willing to pay yet." Gabriel's not my boyfriend, even if he plays the part well. But when I get home, he's going to demand an answer.

Michelle's lips twist. "Okay, well, you know you're already going to do it, right? For your dad." She's switching into her pragmatic mode.

"Probably. Yeah," I admit reluctantly. I'll do anything to get Duncan Wheeler out of that hellhole.

"Okay." She drums her fingers over the tabletop. "So let's figure out what it's going to cost him."

FOUR
GABRIEL

From the corner of my eye, I spot the swirl of jet-black hair. Mercy's home at seven, as I knew she would be despite her attempt to remain aloof and in control through her texts.

I keep my stride in the pool, doing my daily laps, pretending my heart isn't pumping that much harder and that it has nothing to do with the physical exertion.

It's a done deal.

She's mine.

Mercy's already brought all her father's case files to Justin's office. She must have run home the second he left that shithole she works in. I know because I demanded an immediate update and grilled him on everything she said, which sounded like basically everything between "yes" and "please, help me" and "sure, I'll suck Gabriel's cock 24/7 if you get my father out."

But if she wants to keep playing this little game, I'll play, as long as the end result is her naked in my bed every night.

The patio door slides open a few minutes later, and she saunters out barefoot, wearing that same flowery green dress I hiked up this morning. I like her style. Sexy, but not trashy.

She doesn't have to wear bandage-tight dresses to show off her curves.

I ease up to the edge of the pool, resting my arms on the concrete. "Good day?" I ask through my ragged breaths, letting my gaze travel up the length of her slender, toned legs. If she would step just a little bit closer, I might be able to see those panties I peeled off this morning. I wonder if she soaked them, thinking of me all day.

My dick begins to harden with memories of this morning.

She shrugs, feigning nonchalance even as her sharp, dark eyes travel over me. "Just another day."

"So, nothing different about it? Nothing interesting or exciting or ..."

Her eyes narrow. "Justin told you I dropped off the files." She sounds irritated.

"Of course he told me. I'm paying him."

"I haven't agreed to anything," she counters.

I chuckle.

That seems to irritate her even more. "I can just as easily go back there and collect all my dad's files and tell him thanks, but no thanks."

I let myself fall back into the water to float on my back, giving her a full view of my body and the bulge in my shorts. *That's all for you, baby.* "And why would you want to tell him thanks, but no thanks?"

"Because I haven't agreed to anything yet." She folds her arms over her ample chest. "Like I told you, I have terms."

I struggle to smother my smile. "Okay, shoot." She's likely been playing this conversation in her head all day long. This should be fun.

She swallows hard. "How long will this thing between us last?"

"Until I decide it's over." Never, the way I'm feeling right now. Caleb had a woman over earlier for an afternoon swim and fuck. Seeing her naked didn't even faze me. Well, okay, it fazed me. As in, it made me want to drive down to Mercy's work and bend her over her desk. Does she have a desk?

I'm dying to feel her lips around my cock again. And here I thought Lulu was talented in that department. She ain't got nothing on Mercy and that hot mouth of hers.

"No, I need a deadline. It can't be open-ended," Mercy demands, interrupting my dirty thoughts.

"Fine. Until the appeal is sorted or I call it quits. Whichever is sooner."

"The appeal is going to take years."

"So?"

She stares blankly at me a moment. "So what happens when you decide you're bored of me after a month? You're going to keep paying for my dad's legal fees for years after? You expect me to believe that?"

"Yes."

She rolls her eyes.

"I told you, my word is my bond." I swim toward the stairs and climb out of the pool. "Besides, don't be so quick to dismiss how attracted I am to you."

Her penetrating brown eyes drag the length of me. They're hungry. They're always hungry when they're on me. I wonder if she realizes how obvious she is. And how much I like it.

She lets out a slow, soft exhale. "Let's set it at a month, with renegotiation of terms after that point."

"A month," I repeat, mentally tossing that idea around. That's four full weeks. I've never spent four nights with the same woman, so four weeks is probably more than reasonable. Plus, what are the chances that she spends a month living here with all the luxuries I can afford her, in my bed, getting fucked by me daily, and isn't hooked by the end? If she doesn't try to kill me in my sleep, that is. "You're really stuck on this deadline?"

Her jaw tenses. "I need an end date."

I twist my lips, pretending to mull it over. "Fine. One month. And then we renegotiate." I let my gaze slide down her body, imagining it naked. I'm going to make sure she can't get enough of me by the end of that month.

She sets her jaw as if steeling her nerve. "And I want my father's legal fees in an untraceable account that only I have access to. Enough to cover whatever Justin's going to cost for the full appeal."

I feel my eyebrows spike. I wasn't expecting that. I'm impressed. "Do you have any idea how much money that is?"

She gives me a tight-lipped smile in return.

"Who says you're not going to just take the money and run? Why should I trust you?"

"Because my word is my bond," she echoes in a mocking tone. "Besides, where would I go that you couldn't find me or my father?"

True. She's definitely been thinking through this. Has she thought about what she'll do if I say no to this term? I could, easily.

I should.

Then she'd have to swallow her pride and submit to me anyway, because I know there's no way she'll not do whatever is necessary to get her father help.

I *could* be a dick. And if this were anyone else, I *would* be a dick.

"What if something happens to you?" she rushes to say, and I sense a hint of desperation in her tone, as if she can read my thoughts. "What if you can't keep your word because you get into some sort of trouble? The kind that people in the Easton family might get into? Then I'm screwed and my dad's screwed, despite your best intentions."

The kind of trouble that someone involved in drug trafficking could get into, she's saying. As in jail.

Or dead.

Obviously, she didn't buy the lie I fed her last night. And, given the coming volatility, she might have just painted a fair scenario. Caleb's right—if we don't play this smart, we're going to earn our father's wrath, and there's no telling what he'll do.

The thought of leaving Mercy helpless—of not keeping up my end of this—has my stomach turning queasy. "I'll have the funds in an account by tomorrow." I can't believe I'm doing this. If Caleb finds out, I'll never hear the end of it.

Mercy can't seem to believe it either. A look of shock crosses her features before she smooths them over. "Untraceable."

"Of course."

She gives the smallest of nods. "And Justin's agreed that this will look like pro bono."

"Did he now?" Bastard will probably cook his books and weasel some sort of charity grant out of this, if that's even a thing. "That's fine. He's getting paid enough to say whatever you want him to."

She shakes her head, her eyes wandering over the expanse of night sky and city lights below, glowing bright now that the sun has set, before settling on me again. Studying me as if I'm a puzzle she can't piece together. "You could have anyone you want. Why are you going through all this trouble for me?" There's a hint of vulnerability in her voice now.

"How could I not?" It's the truth. I've been inside her three times, and I'm aching with the need to feel the inside of her again. I need to hear her vulnerable cries and feel her inner muscles clamp down around my cock, to see her fall apart despite her determination to not want me. How could any man who's had this woman ever move on? I can see why that lunatic was obsessed with her. He's lucky her dad killed him. If not, I would have.

But, I'm not sure anymore that it's just my physical addiction to her that has me jumping through hoops like a show poodle.

Mercy swallows hard before meeting my gaze. "There are a few more things you have to agree to."

"Of course there are." The account and the end date were the biggies; the things she wanted off her chest right away, the deal makers or breakers. Now let the fun and games begin. Just to add to my entertainment—and her struggle—I shuck my wet trunks and stroll over to sink into the lounge chair, tucking my hands behind my head in a relaxed pose. If there's one thing I do love about summer nights in the desert, it's that you never need a towel. "Such as?"

She fights the urge but loses, her gaze dragging down the length of my body to settle on my dick. It's just standing there, stiff and saying hello, beckoning her to come and sit on it. And by the heat swirling in her eyes, I'm guessing she's picturing what that would feel like. How long did she replay this morning's garage fuck session? As many times as I did through the day?

Did her pussy ache while she was doing whatever it is that she does at that job of hers?

Her eyes flip up to meet mine, and she sees my knowing smile. She hardens her jaw, switching back to business mode. "No other women."

I expected this one. "For me or you?"

"For either of us. But definitely for you."

"But what if I'm in need and you're not around?"

"I'm serious, Gabriel," she says evenly. "I can't be with you if I think you're also with other women. Not if you care whether I enjoy myself. I'm not one of these dick-swappers you like to surround yourself with."

No, you definitely aren't. I told her this morning point-blank that I don't want any other women, but I'm not about to start serenading her with whispers of undying love. "Well, like you said, I've already fucked half of Phoenix's female population. Clearly I haven't found what I want with promiscuity, so maybe monogamy is the way to go." I shrug, feigning indifference. "No other women."

"Not even rubbing sunscreen on naked bartenders on Sunday afternoons."

"She had bottoms on," I counter.

"Would you like me putting sunscreen on Caleb or those twins?"

My shoulders tense at the thought of Mercy's hands on another man. Point taken. "No touching women for any reason."

She studies me another long moment as if assessing the truth in my words and then, seemingly satisfied, says, "Okay."

"But no men, either."

Her perfect eyebrow arches. "For you or me?"

I laugh. "I don't swing that way, baby. But I've seen the way you look at my brother."

"As if I'd ..." She trails off with a bark of laughter, but then she raises her hands in a sign of surrender. "Okay. Fine. I'll give you that concession, as hard as it may be for me to restrain myself." She pauses. "And no shows for him or anyone else."

"What about for me?" I stroke myself from root to tip once, relishing in the way her eyes follow the move. "What if I ask you to put on a show for me? You're not going to be shy, are you?"

Her lips twitch. "Depends on my mood."

"You didn't think you were in the mood this morning in my garage, did you? And then I put you on your back and had you crying my name in about a minute."

Her cheeks flush. "It was early. You caught me off guard."

"And I'll bet if I slipped my hand between your thighs right now, you'd be soaking wet for me." Damn, I've never wanted to fuck a woman so bad in my life as I do every time she's near me.

She adjusts her stance, and I'll bet her pussy's aching with my words. "No shows for anyone else," she repeats, swallowing hard, her eyes flickering to my hand on my dick. "I'm not going to be a star in your home movies either." She gestures at the security cameras.

"I'll make sure to shut that one off when I'm fucking you out here." I don't miss her sharp inhale over my emphasis on the word *fucking*. "What else?" Because my balls are aching something fierce.

She levels me with a hard gaze. "Stop lying to me about

who you really are. What you and your brother do to have all this." She waves dismissively at our house.

My eyebrows arch. That, I was also not expecting. "I don't know what you're talking about," I begin, keeping my voice even. "Caleb and I earn our money from Empire—"

"Just stop." She holds a hand up to stay my words. "Here's my deal—I won't ask, because my guess is that it's better for everyone involved that I don't know anything. But stop treating me like some fool who doesn't know or doesn't care what's going on." Her jaw tenses. "I don't like being lied to, and I have a pretty damn good idea what's going on. I'm just choosing to ignore it for my own gain. That's what I need to do to stomach this."

"Okay. Don't ask, don't tell. That's a deal I can work with." It's the only deal I can work with because Mercy definitely can't learn the details. That would put her and us at risk.

She swallows hard. Was she hoping I'd deny being involved in the dirty drug business again?

"Is that it?" I ask.

"No. One more thing. My father can never find out about any of this. About who's paid for DeHavilland, about me and you, about this deal." Her eyes fall to the ground for a minute, but not before I see the flash of shame in them. Is it shame over lying to him? Or for agreeing to this arrangement with me?

Or because she's associated with the likes of me in the first place?

I'm not surprised about that last one—I'd expect as much from a woman like Mercy—and yet it bothers me far more than I want it to. It makes me want to admit all my sins, beg her forgiveness, and promise her that I'm seeking some sort of redemption. Or at least tell her that I'm trying to change.

"He won't find out from me," I say solemnly. "Is that all?"

She bites her bottom lip. She looks so goddamn sexy doing it that my dick jumps in my palm. "You said you had terms too?"

"One or two." That I've been toying with all day.

Sliding a patio chair out, she gingerly settles into it. She releases a deep breath, as if bracing herself for impending doom. "Okay. Go ahead."

"You'll agree to whatever I want to do, without complaint."

She blinks, looking as if I'd slapped her. "You've got to be kidding—"

"When we're fucking," I clarify, emphasizing that last word. "I kind of dig it when you put up a fight otherwise. But whatever I want from that hot, tight body of yours, I get. Understood?"

Her eyes widen warily. "I'm not into fetishes and pain and all that shit."

"Neither am I," I assure her. "But I'm guessing I like it dirtier than you're used to."

She eyes me as she mulls that over. What I would do to be able to read her mind right now. "What exactly does that mean?" she finally asks.

"You'll have to wait and see. Trust me though, none of it will hurt you." I level her with what I hope is a convincing look. "And you'll be asking for it again by the time I'm done."

A flare of curiosity flashes across her gorgeous face before she smooths her expression. "As long as it doesn't hurt me."

I'll take that as your first yes.

My balls tighten with anticipation. The things I'm going to do to this woman ... "What I want, *whenever* I want it," I clarify.

Her chest rises with a deep inhale, and it seems like she might battle that demand. After a moment though, she offers a solemn nod.

"Are you on birth control?"

"I have an IUD," she admits.

Thank fucking God. "My blood test results should be back tomorrow." It's a miracle what slipping cash into pockets can do for modern medicine. But that's how desperate I am to go bareback with this woman. "As soon as you see that I'm clean, I'm coming inside you." I've never had sex with a woman without a condom before. I can't wait to feel Mercy's wet heat, skin to skin.

She swallows hard and when she speaks again, her voice has taken on a husky tone. "Fine. As long as you don't go near another woman."

She seems to like this idea as much as I do. A rush of blood swells my cock. I didn't think I could get any harder, but here we are. "I already promised I wouldn't. Also, outside of your obligations to your job and schooling, if I ask you to come with me somewhere, you'll be there. I'll be at Empire this weekend and I want you there."

"The *whole* weekend?"

"Evenings only."

She shakes her head. "I have to study this weekend. I have finals next week, and I've worked too hard for too long to fail. I should be studying right now instead of being here, negotiating my sex slavery with you, especially since I got *nothing* done last night."

Because she was too busy taunting me with that sexy ass

in the shower. Right. "You're finished next week?" I'm not used to getting involved with students and having to consider things like schoolwork.

Then again, I'm not used to getting involved with anyone, period. I'm treading all kinds of new water with Mercy.

"Yes. And my standings aren't fantastic, given everything that's gone on with my dad. My one prof was sympathetic at first, but he's run out of fucks to give." Her face pinches with stress.

A surge of anger courses through me at the thought that a teacher would give Mercy a hard time, especially knowing what she's gone through. "Do you want me to have my guys pay him a little visit? Make sure he gives you a passing grade? I have no problem doing it."

She rolls her eyes but then laughs. At least she thinks I'm kidding.

"Fine. Just Thursday night for this week."

"I volunteer at group therapy on Thursdays."

I give her a knowing look. "Until midnight?"

"No," she admits reluctantly.

"Good. So you can meet me at the club after."

She shakes her head and sighs, and I can tell she'll relent to that one night. "Why do you want me there?"

I shrug. "Maybe I like seeing you in a short dress. You can bring your blond friend with you."

She huffs. "Fine. But I'm going to finish my assignment now. And eat, because I'm starving." She wraps her arms around her waist as if to emphasize that.

I've got something for you to fill your mouth with right here.

I give my dick another slow, teasing stroke, and her lips part, a small sigh escaping them. She seems to like that visual. "Are you sure you don't feel compelled to help me out here before analyzing the human psyche, or whatever it is you're doing for school?"

She hesitates, her brown eyes skittering south to my obvious dilemma. "Is this a 'whenever I want it' test?"

Yes. Damn, how easy would it be to demand her mouth around my cock right now? And, by the flash of desire in her eyes, I'm almost thinking she's looking for me to give her an excuse. I've been waiting all day, and right now I want to demand that she spend the entire night riding my lap.

"You should go and eat," I grit out. "There's a plate sitting in the fridge for you, if Caleb hasn't inhaled it yet. Go, and get your assignment done."

She stands and takes a step toward me, but then stalls. "Carnitas, you said?"

"The very best. Caleb ate them all last night, so Rosita made a second batch."

Her searing gaze rakes over me once more before she turns and strolls away. "Enjoy playing with yourself," she calls out, her head held high, her smile triumphant.

FIVE
MERCY

Gabriel has no idea how hard it was for me to walk away from him.

Even now, as I stand in his bedroom, inhaling the aroma of these carnitas—they do smell better than anything I've had in a long time—I watch his sleek, powerful form cut through the water, having picked up where he left off with his laps, and I know there's no way I'm going to be able to focus on this assignment. I can't even focus on eating.

My appetite is for something entirely different, and I am famished.

Damn that bastard, stripping and stretching out on the chair like that. It's like he climbed right into my brain, pulled out that erotic Ambien-induced dream, and reenacted it. All I could think about was mounting his lap.

Michelle helped me wrap my head around what I'd need from him to accept his offer. Some of my demands were deal breakers, and some were far-fetched. I'm bowled over at the fact that he agreed to all of them. Or so he says, anyway. We'll see if he can keep his dick out of his female staff. But I was so sure the money account would be a no-go, that he'd refuse and then I'd be forced to yield to him anyway, because there's no way I'll give up the kind of lawyer he's dangled in front of me. I know it and Gabriel damn well knows it.

But he showed me a kindness.

And another one, by not demanding I blow him right there when he clearly needed the release. Under our new terms, if he had demanded it, I would have had to comply because I'm his. Whenever, whatever.

The very situation I've been so desperate to avoid.

And yet I was flush with want as I started playing out various scenarios of what Gabriel could possibly mean by wanting things dirtier than I'm used to. I may not trust the man, but I trust he knows what he's doing with my body.

Gabriel is a puzzle I can't begin to figure out. The way he lured me into this mess in the first place shows a man devoid of all basic morals and yet he seems to care that I have everything I could possibly need or want. I wonder if that's genuine concern or simply to maintain control of me.

It's best that I keep reminding myself of who he is, before I do something stupid, like start to want more than just his dick.

He is an Easton. The Easton family is involved in crime, and if there's one thing every crime syndicate is involved in, it's illicit drugs. No matter what lies he has told me, I know his family is into drugs.

Yet, he *is* using that money to help an innocent man—my father—get a second chance. For his own perverted gain, of course, but still.

Michelle said I just need to focus on what I'm getting out of him and I'll be fine.

Right now, what I need is relief for the ache between my legs.

Abandoning my dinner for the time being, I fish the bikini I earlier rescued from my apartment out of my bag and change in the bathroom, and then head back outside. Music pumps over the outdoor speakers.

"Thought you had an assignment to work on?" Gabriel calls out midstroke as I round the edge toward the stairs, stepping over the shorts he dropped, and I swear I hear amusement in his voice.

"I felt like a swim to cool off first." His naked body is strong and rippling with muscle and looks especially beautiful against the purplish glow of the pool lights. "Do you do laps every day?" He'd just come from a swim yesterday when I came back after class.

"Great way to stay in shape." He launches himself off the far wall and swims toward me. "The lap pool was a selling feature when we bought this—What the fuck happened to you?" He's on his feet, charging through the last few feet of water with powerful strides, his hard gaze on my legs.

"What are you talking about?" I panic, following his eyes. And then I realize where his focus is—on the dark fingerprints marring my skin. I let out a laugh. "Are you kidding me? These bruises? They're from *you*. Remember, this morning?"

"From me?" Tension still radiates from him. "Did I hurt you? Are you hurt?" he demands to know.

Seeing the horror in his eyes surprises me. His family has no doubt killed people. For all I know, Gabriel himself has hurt people—though he's joked about having "guys" to send messages. Yet, he seems horrified by the idea that he bruised my thighs during our heated morning sex?

I *could* fuck with his head right now and tell him that my legs ache to touch, that I've been sore all day, but I find myself wanting to ease his conscience instead. Taking two steps down to reach him, I smooth a hand through his hair, pushing it back. "I'm fine. I just bruise easily."

His shoulders sink, but his face is still serious as he moves in, blocking my path forward. "You're sure I didn't hurt you?"

"I'm sure." I press my fingertip against one, then another. "See? It doesn't hurt."

He leans in to lay a soft kiss against the darkest of the bruises, his lips cool from the water and yet searing hot against my skin. "I didn't mean to be so rough with you."

I smirk. "Yes, you did."

He sighs, his jaw growing taut. "Yeah, I guess I did." He peers up at me with earnest eyes. "But I won't do it again."

I hesitate. "What if I want you to?" The memory of this morning—of every muscle in his beautiful body straining with exertion, his face twisted with ecstasy—fueled my entire day. I don't want him suddenly turning soft on me.

Fire flashes in his eyes. He holds my gaze as he slides wet, strong hands up the backs of my thighs, cupping either side of my ass, squeezing. "Did you enjoy it?"

"Yes," I admit, heat pooling between my legs as I watch Gabriel's lips move from bruise to bruise, his face floating oh so close to where I'm aching for him to bury it.

I let out a sigh. I can't wait to kiss those lips again.

"New bathing suit?"

"No. I grabbed it when I went back to my place today for my dad's case files."

His fingers skim my skin, settling on the strings of my bikini bottoms. "I don't want you going back to that apartment without me. It's not safe."

I feel the tug. "Hey!" I press my hands over his, stopping him from unraveling the ties completely, my heart racing. "I told you I'm not starring in any home movies."

He drags the tip of his tongue up along my inner thigh and my pulse begins to race. "I already shut the camera off."

"No, you didn't." I steal a glance at the one angled this way, but I can't tell.

"I did. From my phone, while you were inside. I knew you'd be back."

He definitely turned the music on, so I guess it's possible. Still … "I don't believe you."

"Why are you arguing with me about this?"

"I thought you liked me arguing with you," I retort, earning his laugh. "And you didn't *know* I'd come back, you *hoped*."

"How was dinner?" He smirks. "You must have shoveled it in to get back out here so quickly."

"It was delicious." The meal is sitting in the bedroom getting cold as we speak, and the smug bastard knows it.

"You know what else is delicious?" His mouth moves over the material of my bottoms. He presses the flat of his tongue up my center, teasing right where my clit is beneath.

I part my legs on impulse, which earns his dimpled smile.

"Remember what I said about getting what I want, *whenever* I want it?" His eyes glow with promise, his fists bunching around the sides of my bottoms.

He wants me *now*.

With a hard swallow, I remove my hands.

The strings on my bottoms offer no resistance, unraveling with ease when he tugs them a touch harder, the skimpy material falling to the step.

"You have the sexiest body I've ever laid eyes on." Gabriel takes a long, lingering look at the smooth skin he's uncovered, as if deciding where he wants to attack first. "I want to put my mouth on every square inch of it."

I hold my breath, waiting for him to dive in between my legs face-first as he seems to like to. But instead, he weaves his fingers through mine and takes a step back, leading me into the pool until I'm standing before his towering, naked form, looking up into molten eyes.

Kiss me. I project the soft plea with my gaze.

His attention drops to my mouth and I think I've won, until he whispers, "Turn around." His hand finds my hips to help guide me around. "You're overdressed."

I feel a sharp tug on the strings of my top and then the rest of my bikini is falling off, leaving me naked, the warm night air caressing my pebbled nipples. Oddly enough, I'm not self-conscious out here. It's private enough, in Gabriel's wing of the house, on top of the mountain, with no neighbors overlooking. That we have the house to ourselves certainly helps.

"Do you know what I've been thinking about doing to you all day?" He leans in to caress the curve of my neck with his lips. His words alone would be my undoing, delivered in that naturally raspy voice.

I close my eyes and revel in his hard length pressed against my back, resisting the urge to reach back and stroke it. I don't want him to know how much I want him just yet. "I'm sure you're going to tell me."

His hands slide from my hips to my ass to massage each cheek in slow circles, pulling my flesh apart with every pass in a deliberate way, exposing my sensitive skin to the refreshing water. "I think I'd rather show you." He coaxes me forward toward the stairs. "Kneel on the top step." His voice is soft but commanding.

My stomach stirs as I find myself obeying without question. Maybe out of curiosity, maybe out of desire. Likely both.

He comes up behind me. Strong, calloused hands slip between my thighs, persuading my legs apart. Farther, and farther, until they're stretched the full width of the steps and I have to brace myself on the edge of the pool using my hands.

Tonight is already so different from last night. Last night, I still had control, or at least the illusion of it.

I've lost all control to Gabriel tonight.

And a part of me doesn't care.

He smooths his palm back and forth over my sex slowly, teasingly, making sure to stroke my clit with each pass of his forefinger. "Have you been thinking about me all day?"

"Maybe for a minute or two," I lie.

He chuckles. "You just can't admit that you want me, can you?"

"I guess you'll have to find out." I close my eyes and happily wait for the intrusion.

After five more torturously slow passes of his palm, Gabriel pushes two fingers deep inside me.

My lips part with an inaudible sound as I roll my pelvis against his hand.

"Fuck yeah, baby." Gabriel settles his free hand onto the small of my back, pressing down, urging me forward. "Bend over more."

My stomach stirs with a twinge of nerves as I settle my elbows over the hard pavement. I'm utterly exposed in this position.

"You are *so* sexy," he murmurs, his fingers still working while his free hand smooths over my ass, kneading my flesh. If there's one thing Gabriel isn't, it's shy about complimenting my body.

A moment later I feel the first swipe of his tongue along sensitive flesh and I tense.

"Come on, Mercy. I told you I wanted every square inch of you," he whispers.

Taking several deep breaths, I will myself to relax. I did agree to give him whatever he wants. And last night, when I let him explore a bit, when I let him invade this part of me, I came harder than I ever have before. If this is what he wants …

"That's it, baby. Remember how much you loved me touching you here?" His soft words in that crooning voice are my undoing as that silver tongue swirls over me again and again, all while his fingers work their magic, building tension that I crave a release from.

Heat floods toward my center.

"Look how wet you're getting. I knew you'd like that," he growls, sucking and teasing and that spot on my body that I've *never* let anyone go near. He hooks his arms around my thighs and angles my hips to give him better access.

I bite my bottom lip as he indulges like a man starved, his tongue lapping and sliding, and dipping deep inside, only to then shift and toy with my other entrance, prodding at it relentlessly. And repeat. It's overwhelming and intoxicating. I press my forehead to my forearms, his name a whispered moan on my lips as tension begins to build along my spine. This man's skill and passion is unparalleled, his boundaries nonexistent.

And he's right. I *am* enjoying the way he seems to worship my body. I can't brace myself against anything but I manage to roll my hips, angling onto his tongue where I want him, reveling in the feel of his stubble as a tingle builds along my spine.

"That's it, baby. Let me hear you scream." His

voice vibrates through me, setting off my orgasm in a flood, every muscle tensing as his tongue buries deep inside.

"Gabriel!" I rasp as wave after intense wave hits me, my thighs quivering as my body rocks against his face. I chase after every last tremor, my mind going utterly blank for a moment. When the last one subsides, I fall limp, my forehead pressed against my forearms. I can't find the energy to be modest.

"Told you you'd like it," he whispers, his hard pants blowing across my sensitive flesh. He releases my hips and guides my body down into the water, only to maneuver me around and lift me again. I end up back on the steps but straddling Gabriel's lap.

I'm about to tell him that I need a few minutes to recuperate but he simply pulls me in close, his skin radiating heat as he curls his muscular arms around me in an affectionate way. I nestle against him, wrapped up in postcoital bliss.

But between my legs, just beneath the water line, his jutting cock presses against my slit. I study the swollen length now. He's the most well-endowed man I've ever been with, and that he knows how to use his dick is a bonus I haven't fully appreciated yet.

No wonder he's so damn cocky; he has reason to be. And yet he didn't try to fuck me first. He was more focused on getting me off. That's been the case, thus far, with every sordid encounter between us. It's another ill-suited puzzle piece to the selfish, narcissistic version of Gabriel I was so sure I had pegged. *This* version is nothing like the one that sat across from me at Fulcort, eyeing me like a predator eyes its prey.

"See something you want?" he whispers, flashing a

mischievous look my way before dipping down to seize a nipple within his teeth.

I hiss with the sharp pinch, but it's followed closely by a playful, soothing lick.

"That mouth of yours is something else." I smooth my fingertips along his hard jawline, watching him suckle.

"Wait. Was that ... Did you just actually compliment me?" he teases, offering me a dimpled smile before I feel another pinch of his teeth. "This is a first."

"Don't get used to it." I push my hands through his mop of wet hair, getting a firm grip so I can gently angle his head back. Even in the dimness, his beauty catches me off guard for a moment.

His dark eyes narrow. "What's going on inside that pretty little head of yours?"

"I'm just thinking that I should kiss you to shut you up." I lean in to capture his plump lips with mine, in a slow, searing kiss, much like the one he gave me this morning, as we were parting for the day.

He lets out a soft moan.

"Who knew a jerk like you'd like kissing so much," I whisper.

"I don't. But I like kissing *you*," Gabriel admits, his tongue prodding my mouth open to slip inside and stroke mine languidly. But then he pulls back. "But right now I need this sexy mouth of yours elsewhere."

I try not to appear too eager, shifting to sit on the second step, between his powerful thighs. Gabriel leans back to settle on his elbows, his legs splayed, his dark eyes intense as he watches me lean forward. I tease his tip with my tongue, tasting the saltiness already beading.

"Please, baby," he begs, his head falling back, his Adam's apple jutting out. "It hurts."

"I guess you *have* been patient." I close my mouth over his cock and take him in deep with my first dip, sucking hard on the way back up.

"Fuck," he groans. "How did you get so good at that?"

"You really want me to answer that?" I give his smooth, fat tip another teasing swirl.

"No. Don't. It'll just make me really angry and want to kill someone."

"Careful, or you're going to start sounding like a jealous boyfriend."

There's a moment's pause and then he asks, "Would that be so bad?"

"That's not what this is." I take him in again, opening up my throat.

He lets out a deep, guttural cry that carries into the quiet night, and then reaches down to grasp the back of my head. Normally, I'd smack away the hand of any guy doing this, but with Gabriel, I find that I like his fingers firm and tangled in my hair.

I settle into a steady rhythm, my eyes drifting upward over his sexy naked body, his muscles rippling, his pecs two perfect mounds, to catch his eyes watching me intently, unbridled lust shining in them.

This is what he asked for in the first place, in the parking lot that day that I slapped him. Here I am, giving him what he wanted.

And enjoying it immensely.

Life really is ironic sometimes.

In minutes, the urgency of Gabriel's hand increases, and his breathing turns ragged and his hips begin their soft thrust, and I know he's not going to last long.

He lets out a guttural moan a second before the first stream of hot, salty cum shoots down my throat, his length pulsing against my tongue with each stream, filling my mouth.

I release him with a gentle kiss against his tip and let the heavy member fall against his stomach with a slap. He's still hard.

Gabriel brushes away damp strands of hair plastered across my forehead with a stroke of his thumb before settling his index finger beneath my chin and urging my gaze to meet his. "Swallow me," he demands softly, following it with a "please."

I consider denying him, holding on to this last semblance of power, however deluded that notion may be.

In the end, I take him all in.

He lets out a soft sigh of contentment, his massive body shifting down to the second step, then the third, to sit next to me. His gaze is sleepy as he burrows his face into the crook of my neck. "You need to eat dinner," he murmurs, pressing a sexy, tongue-laced kiss against my collarbone, his one arm curled around my shoulders, his other hand splayed across my belly affectionately.

"I also need to do my assignment." Right now though, with my limbs wrapped in Gabriel's strength, I'm in no hurry to move anywhere. It's been so long since I've felt comfort like this.

And I could be mistaken, but Gabriel seems in no rush to go anywhere either.

I tip my head back and study the sky, enjoying the quiet, peaceful moment. It's too early for stars, but I saw them that first night, as I was trying to drink my predicament away. When they do show themselves, they'll be spectacular from up here on the mountaintop. "I can see why you and your brother bought this house."

"Yeah ..." He follows my gaze. "I barely ever make it to

my condo downtown anymore. I think it's been about a month now."

"You have a condo downtown too?"

"I have a few places."

Of course he does. "Where?"

"Here and there," he answers evasively. "Mostly vacation properties."

I sense that's all I'm getting from him on that topic. "How long have you and Caleb lived in this house?"

He frowns in thought. "Two or three years now?"

"And why'd you move in with him? If you already have your own place in Phoenix, I mean. Are you two really that close?"

"I don't know. I guess so? Why not live with him up here though? It'd be way too big for just me." He traces my bottom lip with the pad of his thumb. "Why are you asking all these questions all of a sudden?" I could be mistaken but I catch a hint of suspicion in his tone.

I guess someone like him would be naturally suspicious. "Because I'm sleeping with you," I say matter-of-factly. "I just figured ... I don't know *anything* about you and maybe I should." After what I just let the man do to me, I think at least a few questions are fair.

He seems to consider that. "What do you want to know?"

I shrug. "What do you do with your days, besides swim laps and proposition women in prison parking lots?"

"I thought we had a 'don't ask, don't tell' rule."

"Yeah, of course. But I mean, the normal stuff. There must be something normal that you do during the day?"

He trails a light fingertip over my shoulder, making me shiver. "Well, I'm a night owl so I don't usually come to bed until three or four, and I like to sleep in until ten or eleven."

"You were up earlier this morning," I remind him.

"And, damn, was it worth it." He smiles. "But I also had a nap in the afternoon."

I snort. "Rough life."

He laughs, the deep sound making my body tremble with pleasure. There's a casual air growing around us now. It makes me more comfortable. "Do you have any other family besides Caleb and your father?"

"An uncle and a few cousins. That's about it."

"Are you close with them?"

"Not really." His voice is calm, but I sense the sudden tension in his shoulders. I guess I shouldn't be surprised. A family like his must be fraught with problems. They're damn criminals!

"What about your mom?"

"What about her?" His tone turns sharp. I've clearly hit a nerve. It's the same nerve I hit when I mentioned their mother to Caleb.

"Just ... do you see her often?"

"No. Never."

Maybe I shouldn't keep digging for information, but my curiosity gets the better of my judgment. "So, what does she think about your dad being in jail?"

"She doesn't think anything." He takes a deep breath, his severe gaze on the length of the pool. "She passed away when I was ten."

"Oh." My chest swells with empathy. "I'm sorry." Because I truly am. I know what it's like to lose your mother as a child. "Why didn't you mention that earlier?" Like, when we were talking about dead mothers. It's one of those things you mention, a natural tendency to try and relate to a new acquaintance. Unless it's still painful for him to speak about, I guess.

He shrugs. "Not something I talk about."

I hesitate. "How did it happen?"

His jaw tenses. "Car accident." He peels himself away, releasing me from his grip. "Go and eat."

It's an abrupt dismissal, and one that tells me he doesn't like talking about his mother's death, even after all these years. It also makes me wonder if there's more to the story.

But then he sighs. "Come on, Mercy," he coaxes, his tone tempered. He urges me up with a hand on the small of my back. "Get that assignment finished."

With a sigh, I stand.

Gabriel's gaze skates over my nakedness. "You should walk around like this whenever you're here from now on. Drop your clothes at the door. That should be a new rule."

"I guess you should have made that one of your terms then. It's too late now."

He smirks. "There's always next month, when we renegotiate."

That's right, I did agree to that. Next month. A whole month of him—of this. "You'll be bored by then. Besides, do you really want your brother and the twins seeing me naked?" The lights are still off in the house. I wouldn't be strutting around so freely if there was any chance that Caleb might be home.

"It'd be worth it just to watch them die from jealousy. You are just ..." His words fade as his eyes roam shamelessly. "I can't believe you're mine."

I've been ogled by men before, but Gabriel's the first one who makes me feel like *this*. Like I'm a gift from the heavens above, beyond perfect in every way. He must think so, if he's willing to pay this much for me.

But he *is* paying for me.

"My body is yours," I correct him. "For now. But let's be clear, *I* am not yours, and I never will be."

"Whatever you need to tell yourself." The smile he flashes is infuriating. "But a month from now, the last thing you'll be thinking about is leaving me."

I snort. "That would require that I actually care about you."

"And that would be so impossible? You couldn't fall for me?" He's still wearing a smile but there's something odd in his voice now as his gaze settles on my face.

"Come on, Gabriel. Let's be real here about *why* we're together, *how* we got together." Coercion and bribery. Not a healthy start to any real relationship. "I could never love a man like you."

He chews his bottom lip in thought. "Even if a man like me were willing to change?"

"I'll believe that when I see it." And since whatever shady shit he does is below my radar, I'll never know the difference. No ... Gabriel will never have my heart.

He nods, and I can tell he wants to say more about it but decides not to. "You better get moving, or I *will* make you fail that class and I won't feel the least bit sorry about it."

For a split second, I consider sitting back down and discovering what else he has in store for my body. But I don't have time tonight. I climb out of the pool and wrap my towel around myself.

"By the way," he calls out after me, "your dad's out of the infirmary."

"Really?" My heart rate spikes. "How do you know?"

"I called my contact there today. He'll be able to take visitors this weekend."

"Oh, thank God." I was afraid it'd be weeks before I see him again. "Thank you for checking up on him. It means a lot to me." That Gabriel was thinking about me, that I didn't have to ask.

A secretive smile touches his lips. "You're welcome, Mercy."

I hesitate. "And Fleet's cousin? He knows to leave him alone from now on, right?"

Gabriel tips his head back to look up into the night sky, his throat thick, that sharp point jutting in a delicious way, a way that makes me want to drop this towel, climb onto his lap, and drag my tongue along it. While I ride him. "He's learned his lesson."

There's something in Gabriel's voice—an edge—that sends a shiver down my spine, but I quickly push it aside. It doesn't matter what they did to warn that bastard off further retaliation. He deserved whatever Gabriel's "guys" did to him. The important thing is that my dad is safe from being attacked, and he has a kickass lawyer working to get him out.

A deal made with the devil or not, things are *finally* starting to look up for us.

SIX
GABRIEL

"We should go and see this place." I scroll through the pictures of the Mage hotel and casino on my laptop. Howard, our real estate agent, has been scouring possible options for an Empire expansion around the Vegas strip for us: vacant spaces, seedier clubs that could use a new owner and renovation.

He's convinced us to think big. An Empire Hotel and Casino would be huge. The Mage is about to go under, and he thinks we should be ready to jump on it—turn it into the Empire Hotel and Casino, with a club on the rooftop. It's an older place, and it's been poorly managed these last few years, the owner too busy filling his nostrils with white powder and fucking anything that fancies him—both male and female—to see the writing on the wall.

Howard hears this guy's about a month from going bankrupt or overdosing. Possibly both.

It's a big, risky step, and we're well aware that Howard would make one hell of a sales commission on this, which is serious motivation for him to push us toward it. But Howard also knows better than to steer us wrong, so I can't help but give this idea serious thought.

"Dude. A hotel, casino, *and* club? The Feds are already crawling up our asses. Let's just invite them up to the penthouse so they can give us a proper rim job," Caleb murmurs absently, his attention on the front page of today's newspaper. He's religious about keeping up with the goings-on around the city—the politics, the crime, the new business ventures. He may play the idiot playboy, but my brother's actually sharp as a tack.

"Now you're talking." I chuckle. Because that's what opening a Vegas casino would do. Not that there aren't enough disreputable fucks running those places in Vegas right now. So what's one more? "It's not a bad idea though." Especially given I'm trying to turn over a new leaf, one that won't land us in prison.

"Start clean, run clean, and we've got nothing to hide, right?" is Caleb's answer, though it's followed with a small shrug and a sardonic smirk, because the kind of money we'd need to take on a venture like that wouldn't be clean. A lot of it hasn't even been laundered yet. It's sitting in private real estate loans to foreign buyers, waiting for them to either default or sell and clean our money for us. The rest is in offshore accounts, hidden under a multitude of layers and aliases, waiting to be put to good use.

But if we could pull this off, we'd be set for life. A Vegas life, mind you, but it's not like we aren't made for it anyway. We were born and raised in the kind of shade that comes with that seedy world—sometimes the gray areas, many times the outright black areas that you have to be able to thrive in.

We wouldn't need the drug business—let the cartel swim in it—and we could get away from the prison fight circuit. Vegas means gambling and fighting, and gambling on fights. We're experts at all that.

"You know, Mike's heart might explode if we ask him to help us." A club is one thing, but what does the big brute know about hotels and casinos?

"Mike's dick will explode when he sees the kind of money he'll be earning, helping us with this," Caleb throws back. "But taking something this big on would mean one of us living there for a stretch. You willing to live in a Vegas hotel for the foreseeable future? Because I don't know if I am. I'm pretty set here."

He's right, we can't leave that all to Mike, though he'll be a big part of getting us up and running. We'd need an entire staff of reliable managers who know what they're doing, and one of us would need to be there to make sure the millions we're sinking in gets us the return we need.

"Hotel living isn't my thing." I tried it for a summer, back when I was eighteen and floating around Europe. Then again, this would be one location. And we'd own the goddamn hotel. "Plus, I doubt Mercy would be willing to move four hours away while her father is still in prison, which he could be for years."

Caleb's head whips toward me. He pushes his sunglasses down the bridge of his nose to penetrate me with his high-browed stare. "What. The. Fuck. Gabe?"

Shit.

He's right. What the fuck, Gabe is right. This is a woman I've bribed into fucking me, and somehow I've begun planning my life around her?

Last night with Mercy was ... Yeah. It was amazing and we didn't even fuck. And then we sat around and talked, and the truth is, I could have stayed there talking to her all night. Maybe we would have, if she hadn't brought up my mother. That's not a story I want to explain to her. How would she take it?

Would it scare her off?

I wouldn't blame her if it did.

So I sent her away to eat and do her schoolwork, and when I popped my head in later, she was so absorbed with her books and her laptop—looking librarian-sexy with her hair piled on top of her head, the end of a highlighter between her teeth, a studious frown across her forehead—that I did both of us a favor and stayed far away, watching the ball game in the living room.

By the time I ventured in at close to eleven, unable to stay away another minute and hoping for a fuck, she was sprawled out across the bed, passed out. So I *didn't* do what I wanted to do—spread her legs wide and wake her up with my dick—and instead collected her things and tucked her in. Then I went and jacked off in the shower.

I've been acting like a fucking desperate school boy ever since this woman stepped into my life.

And now I'm suddenly talking like I'm thinking marriage.

Mercy sure as hell isn't thinking marriage.

I could never love a man like you.

That's what she said, and even though I expected as much, it stung.

Before Caleb has a chance to lay into me for letting myself get hung up on a woman, the patio door cracks open, and Uncle Peter and Vic stroll out.

"Rosita let us in," Vic says by way of greeting.

Of course she would. They're family. Technically. But we'll need to have a conversation with her about that.

I share a quick glance with my brother and swiftly—but not

too obviously—shut my laptop. No need for them or anyone else, namely our father, to catch wind of what we're looking at doing before we actually commit. They wouldn't approve. It's much easier to fly under the radar with a few ma-and-pop storefronts and lackluster wedding halls than a Vegas high-rise. But this place will have nothing to do with them anyway.

"What do we owe this pleasant surprise to, dearest uncle?" Caleb croons in that tone that drips of condescension and annoys the hell out of our uncle and cousins. My brother has always had a hard time hiding his disdain for Peter. It was our father who sparked the feud with Camillo Perri, cutting into the Perri territory in a dangerous, overt way. But it was Uncle Peter who poured gasoline on the flames—literally—by blowing up their third-generation family restaurant. He didn't know that Camillo's mother was inside, rolling her handmade gnocchi.

At least, that's what he said.

But he knew that the Perris would seek retribution, so he hid his family away, and Camillo Perri decided to cast his net wider. Revenge is revenge, right?

Our mother was the one burned for it in the end. A bloody message to not mess with family. Maybe an attempt to cause a divide between the two sides of the Easton empire, to weaken us so they could move in.

All it did was fuel the war. Camillo knew retaliation was inevitable and so his wife was shuttled away to somewhere unknown for the better part of three years, until I guess he thought tensions may have simmered down.

Gena Perri's Mercedes was run off the road one rainy night, a few miles away from one of the Sonoma vineyards they own, down an especially treacherous escarpment.

Somehow, she survived.

After that, a truce was called for the sake of the children. It's been shaky at best all these years.

And here we are now, thinking about an alliance.

Our cousin Vic wanders over to the edge of the pool, pretending to be absorbed by the view, his hands casually tucked into his pockets. We're not fooled. That short, stocky frame is teeming with tension, as always. At thirty-five, he's the oldest of the Easton boys and generally bitter with life. When he's around Caleb, that bitterness seems to multiply. It's usually because Caleb says something to push his buttons.

Right now though, he's scoping out our surroundings.

"We safe to talk?" Uncle Peter takes a seat across from me under the umbrella and sets his fedora on the table. It's so circa 1920s prohibition era. He and my dad have a matching collection of them. Caleb and I always told our father he's a fool—he might as well walk around with a marquee above his head, an arrow pointing down saying "here I am!"

In a lot of ways, having Uncle Peter sitting across from us is like having our dad here. They're only a few years apart in age, and they look a lot alike—same narrow, cold eyes, same bulging nose and pockmarked skin, same smarmy smirk—though my dad's recent and swift weight gain has dulled the resemblance. Uncle Peter's blond hair turned a wiry gray before my father's did, and it's much thinner but he keeps it tidy and trimmed.

All in all, Uncle Peter looks like a thinner, healthier version of his brother.

With a few strokes on my phone, music streams out of the speakers, just loud enough to muffle recordings should anyone be listening—though my contact at the Bureau hasn't mentioned any surveillance teams on us as of late. "Safe enough," I answer.

"Another one of our associates went missing two nights ago," he begins, studying his manicured hands a moment, one finger on each hand adorned with ornate gold rings. "We can't allow our *problem* to continue."

Our "associates" are the higher-up-the-food-chain dealers—biker presidents, gang leaders like Puff—who we rely on buying big batches that they can then sell at street level. If one went missing, it means the cartel likely got to him. Scared him into buying their product or buried him for refusing. That, or the feds poached them. Either way, it's not good. We need a reliable network to move product.

"I guess your purse is too light this week to worry about your brother meddling in affairs anymore?" Caleb says mildly. Throwing our uncle's words back at him.

"Which means your purse is light, too," Vic throws in with so much poison in his voice, I'm shocked we don't keel over from toxic vapors.

"We have no worries. Empire's doing well," Caleb retorts.

"I'm glad to hear that. Now, perhaps you would consider helping to ensure Harriet keeps doing well. She does keep your father comfortable and allows you the luxury of this lifestyle." Uncle Peter waves his hand around.

Caleb offers an infuriating smile. "*We'd* survive fine without her." But these guys wouldn't. It's no secret that both Peter and Vic have gambling problems and poor business management skills that have cost them a small fortune. Plus, their shitty little side businesses bring next to no revenue. They definitely can't clean their cash fast enough without raising major flags.

Uncle Peter smirks. "If that is true, then why did you come to my house the other day?"

"Because we're loving sons." With a heavy sigh, Caleb folds his newspaper and sets it on the table. "Okay. Please, tell us what you suggest we do to fix that problem, oh wise one? How can *we* help *you*?"

Uncle Peter's lips twist with disdain, but that's the only sign that he's perturbed. I know he'd love to haul back and smash his chunky gold ring across Caleb's face. He and my father are crazy fucks who push respect and loyalty as the family mantra, and Caleb is nothing if not disrespectful.

The thing is, my brother may play the easygoing playboy, but he has a wild, unpredictable temper that has reared its ugly head once or thrice. Who knows what he'd do if Peter actually hit him? Caleb's brain is wired different than mine. It's miswired. It short-circuits when he's angry, and around Peter and our cousins, he's in a state of perpetual simmering rage.

So what would Caleb do if Peter laid a hand on him? Hard to say, but it would likely involve taking his anger out on Vic. My brother's an ass but he wouldn't beat up his aging uncle.

I have a better idea than sitting back and waiting for shit to happen that would put us at war with the other half of the Easton family.

"*It was suggested* that we have a conversation with our old family friends in the valley," I say.

Uncle Peter's manicured eyebrow arches. "Vlad suggested this?"

I give a curt nod.

He seems to mull it over. "United, we stand. Divided, we fall."

"Something like that." I risk a quick glance at Caleb to see him watching me carefully.

Vic wanders over. "Is this smart, given the history?"

Where Caleb's rage simmers for these two men, his hatred for the Perris is a festering volcano.

But Caleb is cunning, and he's figured out why I mentioned the Perris to our uncle just now. "I'd be willing to meet with the two youngest. They had no part in what happened in the past," he begins with an air of reluctance that isn't entirely false, setting the stage for the meeting we need to have with Merrick and Vince. This way, if either Uncle Peter or our father catch wind of it, they'll assume we're meeting to discuss an alliance against the cartel, and not an alliance against them.

Uncle Peter frowns in thought. "And do you really think they'll entertain such an idea?"

"They have as much to lose as we do if we can't get control of this." I doubt the cartel is singling us out. They're equal opportunity assholes.

Uncle Peter looks to his son, who shrugs and then nods in agreement. As if his approval means shit. Fucking cocksucker.

"Okay. Set the meeting up and let us know where to go—"

"We're not your goddamn secretary. We'll make initial contact." Caleb smoothly cuts our uncle off, tacking on a wicked grin. "After all, you blew up sweet little Nonna. I doubt they'd ever be happy to see you."

Our uncle fixes him with a steely gaze. "We aren't agreeing to an alliance without a meeting to discuss terms."

I stifle a sigh. Terms. First Mercy, now these guys.

Though, agreeing on terms with Mercy was a hell of a lot more pleasurable.

"Maybe we don't care if you agree or not," Caleb, always the instigator, throws back.

"Maybe you should start being a bit nicer to us or we'll cut you right out of the equation," Vic hisses. "What the hell do you two really do, anyway?"

"What the hell do we ..." The words fade from Caleb's mouth as he echoes Vic, and I catch the edge in his tone.

Oh shit.

The next few seconds are a blur. Caleb's on his feet fast, his chair toppling over with a crash as his hand closes over Vic's throat.

Vic gets one shot in across Caleb's mouth but it doesn't even faze him. He kicks Vic's feet out from under him, sending our cousin crashing against a side table, smashing the plexiglass on his way down. That isn't enough for Caleb, though. He hauls Vic to the edge of the pool and, dropping to his knees, forces our cousin's head below the water's surface. "I think we've been pretty useful, don't you?" he says through gritted teeth.

"He can't hear you," I warn. It's not the first time I've seen Caleb shove a man's head into a pool. I'm just hoping this time he pulls him up before the air bubbles stop rising altogether, because drowning our cousin will not be good for family dynamics.

Uncle Peter is eerily calm through this. I struggle to match his demeanor. Someone needs to try to keep this visit from turning nuclear. "Let *us* start the conversation, and then we'll bring you all in before anything is decided. It's better to feel them out first and smooth things over, and I think you'll agree that that's our department." The Perris want to scorch the earth Peter walks on, and neither Vic nor Alexei has a charming bone in his body.

"That would probably be wise." Peter's cold blue eyes

flash to the pool, the only indication that he even notices the fight.

"Caleb!" I bark in a sharp warning after a few seconds, hoping I don't have to go over there and physically break it up.

He finally relents, hauling Vic up and releasing him. Vic spends a few minutes sputtering over the pavement. I hope he's not stupid enough to open his mouth and earn himself another round, because my brother could do this all day. For a guy who barely sleeps, his high level of energy is unmatched.

"We'll reach out soon and let you know by the end of the weekend what we come up with," I promise.

"Good." Uncle Peter reaches for his hat. No need for casual chitchat. "You've always been the smart one."

I shoot a warning look my brother's way before he has a chance to answer. We already have the cartel in our backyard, and we're jumping into bed with our enemies. We don't need an all-out war from every angle.

Vic clambers to his feet, his shirt drenched, his face purple with rage.

"Have a nice day." Caleb grins wide at them both, despite his split lip. It's his "I want to beat your face in" grin.

I'm sure Peter has figured that out too. "Say hello to my brother when you see him next." He sets his hat back on his head and then he and Vic disappear through the patio door. Where Rosita is, I have no idea, but my guess is she found a bathroom in the far corner of the house to scrub the second they walked through the door.

"Well, that went well," I mock, glaring at Caleb.

"I don't trust them." He watches the door as if Vic might storm back through and attack at any moment.

"You don't trust anyone."

"I trust you." He licks at his lip, no doubt tasting the coppery tinge of blood. That and his damp arms are the only evidence of his tussle with Vic. Even his breathing is steady. The guy has a crazy switch: on and off, just like that.

I sigh. "Then trust that I know what I'm doing. Think about it. Now we have a cover for the meet if they've got eyes on us."

With a sigh, Caleb sinks into his chair, collecting his newspaper. "You heard what that shithead said, though? Now that Dad's behind bars, they want to cut us out completely."

"That's not a surprise either," I remind him.

"Yeah, well, fuck them if they have the balls to try it. We're not letting them get away with that."

I stifle my eye roll. Caleb wants away from the dirty drug business as much as I do. "That's your ego talking." I flip open my laptop. "Peter or Vic making a move works to our advantage. It'll turn Dad's wrath on them and not on us." Because if Peter pulls a betrayal like this? It'll be a hundred times worse than his sons not carrying on the family business.

And prison walls have yet to shorten Dad's reach. He is one conniving son of a bitch.

"You're right. That'll end worse for them than taking on the fucking cartel." Caleb's chuckle has a sinister quality to it.

"Of course I'm right." And then maybe we can get the hell away from this mess once and for all. Unless Vic and Peter try to bury us in the process. But my brother's worries are fair; we can't trust them with anything.

"Let me see how fast I can get the Perris into town." I slip my burner phone from my pocket and fish the business card Merrick handed me from my wallet.

"Tonight?"

"Nah. Got business up north." Code for another prison circuit match.

"That's right. I heard they dug up some mofo from down south."

"Mad Dog." I hear he's a beast with a hard punch and an affinity for pummeling kidneys. In a no-holds-barred ring where anything goes, that could spell trouble for our cash cow. I need to make sure Chops gets the message. I need to deliver it personally.

"Well, the sooner, the better, as much as I hate the idea of all this." He shakes his head, his gaze on the newspaper, but I can tell he's not actually reading. "We've got family coming at us from one side, the fucking cartel on the other, and now we're climbing into bed with our sworn enemies? We need to know everything we can before we sit down across from them. Where they eat, where they shit, who they fuck. *Everything*."

"Get Stan on it." Our private investigator, a retired cop and shady-as-fuck when it comes to getting us what we need in a timely manner. I don't know how he finds out half the stuff he does, but it's always solid intel. My guess is, laws and basic human rights do not apply to his moral compass.

And that's just fine with us.

"I mean, how do we know the Perris aren't setting us up?" Caleb, ever the suspicious one, says.

"We'll know. *I'll* know," I promise him, adding with a smug smile, "after all, you heard Uncle Peter. I am the smart one."

"You know what, little bro? A week ago, I would have agreed with you. But then you bribed a woman to come live with us and now you're talking the way you are, and I don't know, Gabe." He shakes his head. "What do you got planned next? Have you been shopping for rings yet?"

"Fuck off. Don't even go there." I'm a long way off—like, from here to the moon—from ever so much as considering putting a ring on any woman's finger. Though, if someone put a gun to my head and said I had to choose tomorrow, I could think of far worse things than calling Mercy my wife. The woman is easily my match in intelligence, and she's got guts.

Plus, she is hands down the most beautiful creature I've ever laid eyes on.

"Jesus Christ. Never thought I'd see the day." Caleb shakes his head. "Just make sure nothing else leaks out of you while you're shooting your load into her, like, you know, shit that will land us with dad."

I glare at him. "I'm not an idiot."

"Says the idiot who bribed a woman to fuck him and is now falling for her," he counters with a sarcastic laugh.

"I'm not falling for her."

"'Kay. Let me fuck her tonight."

My stomach churns with just the idea of that. "You so much as touch her and I'll kill you!"

Caleb throws his hands in the air. "Point made."

"Focus, shithead! We've got bigger things to deal with right now." I wave Merrick's business card in my hand and then punch in the numbers written across the back in blue ink.

A flicker of worry darts across my brother's face as we wait for someone to answer the call.

I wonder if we'll ever look back and think ... yeah, this was the moment we signed our death certificates.

SEVEN
MERCY

The night air is muggy when I step out of the campus building on Wednesday night, my books tucked under one arm, the keys to the SUV dangling from my fingertips. There must have been a flash shower while I was inside the lecture hall, listening to Professor Pearson drone on. After so many years of toiling away at this degree, it's getting harder with each class to keep my focus. That could be because I'm so close to being finished.

But now it more likely has to do with what's waiting for me at the other end of my drive tonight.

A mixture of anxiety and excitement courses through my veins at the thought of seeing Gabriel again. He came to bed after I fell asleep again last night, tidying my books for me. He didn't stir in the morning when my alarm went off, and I'd be lying if I said a part of me wasn't disappointed.

That I didn't want to feel his lips on mine before I started my day.

But what will tonight hold for me?

"Hey, Mercy! Wait up!" My classmate Ben, a lanky blond guy, rushes out the doors, panting as if he's been running. "So, you want to meet on Saturday afternoon to study for the exam? You know, so I have a chance at passing?"

I can't help but smile. The only person getting help out of that scenario is me. Ben is super smart and patient, and in the four years since I've known him, I've always done better in the classes we take together. I credit my good grades up until now partly to him. I know he tutors students, but he's never even suggested tutoring—and charging—me.

It's likely because Ben has had a crush on me since the first day I met him, when he spent the entire class ogling me from across the lecture hall. He's never acted on it though, and he's always been sweet if not a little bit awkward, so I don't mind pretending that I don't notice.

"I can't on Saturday. I'm going up to see my dad."

"Right, of course." He pushes a hand through his mop of brown curls. He's only twenty-one, and he looks sixteen. I doubt he shaves more than once a week, if that. "I'm sorry, I forgot. Sunday, then?"

"Sunday could work," I say tentatively, even as my mind churns. Unless Gabriel demands that I'm somewhere. Though, I did tell him that this weekend is for studying, so he can't interfere with that. Besides, weekends are party central at the house—booze and boobs all day long. I'll be better off toiling over books elsewhere.

I can't ignore the twinge of worry that edges in with that thought. Those days mean naked women strutting around, batting their lashes, and holding out bottles of sunscreen. Will Gabriel be tempted by breasts and ass and his brother's deviant behavior? Is this going to be a case of "If Mercy's not there to catch me sticking my dick in someone, did it ever really happen?"

A burn flares in my stomach. Oh God, I'm jealous. I *hate* being jealous.

"Yeah, sure, I think Sunday could work?" I'm not going to be able to study alone with those kinds of questions swirling in my head.

Ben smiles and his whole face lights up. "Okay, cool. Why don't you meet me at the library at eleven? I should be home from church by then and ..." His words trail off, his gaze drifting behind me, his eyes widening. He lets out a whistle. "Someone's got a sweet ride."

I turn in time to see the black Lamborghini pull up to the curb, earning plenty of curious glances from students spilling out of their evening classes.

My heart begins to race before Gabriel even steps out. He's dressed in casual jeans and a soft gray T-shirt, and he somehow makes that look upscale. But what is he doing here? He texted earlier to ask what time class let out and which campus I was at. I assumed it was casual chitchat, not "I'm going to stalk you there later."

He rounds the sports car and leans back against it, folds his arms, and stares up at me, his expression unreadable.

"Do you know that guy?" Ben asks cautiously.

"Yeah. He's ... a friend." What else do I call Gabriel? Ben is not as understanding as Michelle. He's the son of a Baptist minister. I would bet money that he's still a virgin. There's no way he'd understand this mess I've gotten myself into. "I'll text you about Sunday, okay?"

"Sure. Have a good night." His brow furrows as he watches Gabriel, but he says nothing else.

I ease down the steps, my sandals slapping the concrete as I make my way over, trying to decide how I want to receive Gabriel. By the time I'm close enough to inhale his cologne, I've chosen a salty greeting, because it'll stall the overwhelming and unwanted urge to bury my face in the crook of his neck. "What a lovely surprise!" I say in a derisive tone. "Let me guess, you were in the neighborhood."

"Something like that. Who's the twelve-year-old?" His sharp gaze is on Ben, who lingers on the steps, checking his messages on his phone.

"A friend."

"A friend who wants to fuck you."

I roll my eyes. It wasn't a question.

"We agreed to no men."

"You're kidding me, right?" I laugh.

The steely look on Gabriel's face when he meets my eyes says he actually may not be.

"Our agreement has nothing to do with *talking* to people, so don't you dare try to pull this jealous crap with me," I hiss, my anger flaring at this alpha bullshit. "Not unless you want to fire every female staff member you've ever fucked."

Gabriel's eyebrow arches.

"*Exactly*. My guess is there'd be no one left to work at Empire. Ben's a friend. We study together sometimes. In fact, we're studying together this Sunday. And if you even try to—"

Gabriel's mouth crashes into mine in a hard kiss, his tongue pushing in to tangle with mine, stealing whatever words remain. It's fast and forceful, and not appropriate for college curbside, but something tells me Gabriel doesn't care.

At the moment, neither do I.

It's all I can do to keep my books within my grip and my knees from buckling, the heat from Gabriel's hand on my hip searing. Someone somewhere lets out a catcall, and I know it has nothing to do with the car.

When Gabriel finally breaks free, there's a wicked gleam in his eyes. "Every time you scold me, I'm going to do that," he warns in a seductive purr. "And every time I catch another man eyeing you, I'm going to do *this*, so they know you're mine." Reaching around to grip my ass, he yanks me forward, pulling me flush to his body, his hard length pressed against my waist.

"You're crazy." I take a moment to catch my breath.

He smiles, unfazed. "And you are so fucking hot when you're telling me off."

I steal a glance at the steps to see that Ben is already gone.

Gabriel smirks, his hard gaze tracing my lips. "He did the smart thing and left."

"What are you doing here? You couldn't wait until I got back to your place to maul me?"

Finally releasing me, he takes a step back. "Actually, I've got somewhere I need to be tonight. I'm texting you a code to get into the house through the garage," he murmurs, tapping his phone. My phone chirps in my purse a second later.

"Where are you going?" I ask without thinking.

He arches an eyebrow. "Somewhere I highly doubt you'd want to know about."

Don't ask, don't tell. "Never mind. So I guess I'll see you later?"

"I'll be late."

"Oh." An unexpected wave of disappointment hits me.

Gabriel laughs. "Don't worry, baby. I can wake you up when I get home, if you want."

Yes, please. I swallow that request to keep it from escaping. "I'm sure I'll be fine. Especially if Caleb's home," I add with a teasing tone.

"You'd rather chew your own arm off than let my brother's dick anywhere near you, but nice try. Besides, he wouldn't dare."

"Why not? I thought you shared all the time."

"Not you." Gabriel slips a business card out of his back pocket. "I also came to give you this. That thing we talked about last night? It's been arranged."

I scan the front. George Collins. Accountant. This must be about the money for my father's defense. "Really? It's already done?"

"I told you it would be," he says smoothly.

And his word is his bond.

I fumble with the card in my grasp. At the other end of that number is a shit ton of money—I don't know how much —to secure legal help for my dad. Maybe his freedom. At least, I think it is. Could Gabriel be scamming me?

"Call that number, and George will help you get what you need, when you need it. He'll explain what you need to do. Make sure you always speak to him in person though." Gabriel shoots me a warning look. "That's how it'll stay the way you want it."

Untraceable. No emails, no phone conversations. If there's anyone who knows how to hide money, my guess is it'd be the Eastons' accountant.

I tuck the card into my purse. Do I thank him for this? Given what I've had to offer up to get it, is that appropriate?

I feel the overwhelming urge to thank him. I bite down on my tongue to keep it from escaping though, reminding myself who Gabriel is, what he's requiring of me in exchange for this.

I've more than earned every dime.

"You've been busy today," I say instead.

He smiles. "I have." He pulls out a slip of paper from his shirt pocket and hands it to me.

Curiously, I unfold it, to find a printout of Gabriel's blood test results.

He may have slept with countless women but he's clean.

Which means that the next time we have sex, he's coming inside me. My inner muscles clench in anticipation of that. Why does the idea of that turn me on so?

Again, I see that little devilish twist of his lips, like he knows my secret. "Well. I should go. I've got a bit of a drive and I can't be late." Gabriel says this but he doesn't make a move, his dark eyes wandering over the campus building. "So this is what college looks like."

"You never went?" I literally know *nothing* about this man.

"Me? College?" He chuckles. "Nah."

"Why not? You seem like a smart guy. You could have gotten in."

"I am smart. Smart enough to know I don't need to waste my time here."

"Yeah, I guess not. Not with your mountain of hard-earned money to play with."

He smirks at my sarcasm. "Plus I can afford to hire other smart people to do all the work for me. See you later, baby." He leans in to graze my jawline with his lips, lingering there a few beats before he finally strolls toward the Lambo's driver side, ignoring the many curious gazes still on us.

"Hey!" I call just as he's about to disappear inside. "Why'd you come?"

He frowns. "What do you mean?"

"I mean you texted me the code to get into your house,

and those other two things could have waited until later. So, why'd you come here tonight?"

He opens his mouth to answer and falters, an odd, unreadable expression flashing across his face. "Like you said, I was in the neighborhood."

I bit my bottom lip to hide the smile that's threatening to escape. No, he wasn't. He just wanted to see me tonight. Knowing that brings a thrill that I don't want to feel.

A sexy dimple pops with his smirk. "I'll see you when I get home." He climbs into his car and, with a rev of the Lambo's engine, he speeds off for the night.

When I'm sure he can no longer make me out in his rearview mirror, I let the goofy grin emerge.

EIGHT
GABRIEL

It's almost 3:00 a.m. by the time I walk through my bedroom door.

Mercy left the blinds open, allowing the moonlight to stream in. It casts a glow over her still form, draped in the silky white sheet.

She looks too peaceful to wake.

I've been rock-hard the entire drive home, imagining how good the inside of her is going to feel, how thrilling it's going to be to unload inside of her for the first time.

I'm also in serious need of a shower, I accept, looking down at the dried blood on my hands and my shirt. Chops was leaking from a dozen spots by the time the fight was over, despite the lowdown I gave him about his opponent. This Mad Dog guy came from the bowels of hell—apparently he survived ten years in a Mexican prison before coming back to America to commit a slew of crimes that would guarantee he'd end up in our prison system. Whatever he learned in the Mexican prison he put to good use, because even a guy like Chops couldn't shake him off. He really did fight like a mad dog after the last bone on the planet.

Chops still won, but not without plenty to stitch up and nurse back to health. There was a point during the bout when everyone was holding their breath and I was sure he was going down and not getting back up. He could barely make it out of there on his own two feet, and I left him in the infirmary tonight, peeing blood. He even passed on Joyce, his prize hooker, so I know it's bad.

Now I'm left wondering if I should be driving down to Tucson and convincing Mad Dog that he needs to be *our* mad dog. We'll sure as shit line the prison guards' pockets with more cash than the guy who speaks for him—a punk named Ronny whose daddy owns a grocery chain and is dabbling in the underworld like a toddler dabbles with finger paint.

After tossing my ruined shirt in the trash and washing away a long day of filth under the warm spray of the showerhead, I ease into my king-sized bed, pausing to admire the mass of jet-black hair that fans out over Mercy's pillow.

It was around six when I decided that I needed to find her on campus, after her class, and before I had to head to the match. She's right, I had no legitimate reason to.

I just needed to see her.

I needed to feel her supple body against mine, to taste her sweet lips, smell her silky skin, even if for only a few minutes.

I needed to insinuate myself in her life.

When I saw that fucking little shit mooning all over her on the stairs, I nearly lost it. I've never been jealous like this over a woman. Hell, I've watched my brother and the twins fuck women that I just finished with and there's never been so much as a twinge of bitterness. Nothing, nada.

With this guy, I had this flash in my mind of grabbing the Glock that's tucked under my seat and darting up the stairs to shove it in his face, make him piss his pants whenever he so much as accidentally glances Mercy's way again.

But then Mercy called me on my shit, and I went from burning with jealousy to ready to bend her over the hood of my car.

Since then, coming home to her in my bed is all I've been able to think about—aside from the few brief moments of wondering if Chops was going to die, of course.

Now, listening to her shallow breaths, inhaling that floral scent of her skin and hair, the nicer side of me tells myself that I should let her sleep—she has to be up in three hours after all. But the selfish side—the one sporting eight inches of wood that needs a release—shifts over to ease in behind her tight, slender body, intent on—

She's naked.

I hiss with excitement as I feel her bare, hot skin against mine. She went to bed without her usual boxers and tank top.

If that isn't a sign that she wants me to wake her up ...

I smooth a hand over her hip, admiring her shapely curves.

"What time is it?" she whispers sleepily. The woman must be running on fumes at this point, after all she's been through with her father, plus trying to keep going with life. No wonder she's passing out before she can put her books away at night.

I should let her sleep. Too bad my self-centered side will always win out. That side is why she's here in the first place.

"It's time for me to make you feel good." I press flush against her, letting my cock line up with the crack of her ass. I can't wait to take that. Not tonight though. Tonight, I want to look into her eyes when I sink into her. I want her to curl her arms and her legs around me; I want her lips on mine.

"I didn't take you for a cuddler," she murmurs, a teasing smile in her sleepy voice.

"Is that what you call this?" I hook a hand around her leg and guide her thighs apart, angling my hips to fit between them. My cock slides through her slick folds, earning her soft sigh.

"Are you ever not hard?" Her limbs are relaxed, offering no resistance.

"Around you? No." I burrow my face into her tangle of raven-black hair, inhaling the intoxicating scent. "Are you ever not wet?" I hold my breath and wait for her to wake up fully and bristle, to deny that I make her horny because she's too stubborn to admit it, even though I can feel glaring evidence to the contrary.

"Around you?" She sighs, almost with reluctance. "No." She shifts her body a touch, giving me better access to between her legs.

"I like you half asleep. You're less prickly."

"I thought you liked me prickly."

"I think I might like you sweet even more." Normally, I enjoy foreplay but at this hour I don't have the patience. Also, my balls hurt. "You're going to start sleeping naked every night from now on." I guide her hips until she's flat on her back and then climb on top of her.

"Am I, now?" she purrs, her hands settling onto my shoulders, smoothing over them affectionately, as if memorizing their shape.

I pause to study her face in the moonlight. "You're an angel." Like, a goddamn angel handcrafted by Zeus or some shit. Her body is literally perfect—her skin creamy and smooth, her legs long and slender, her nipples symmetrical pale pink discs, her breasts firm, high, and full, her torso long, her stomach flat.

The heaven between her legs is the tightest, pinkest spot on earth.

She shows it to me now, parting her thighs wide, beckoning me with a demure smile.

And that look on her face?

That's the look of a woman who desperately wants it and, for once, isn't hiding that fact from me.

Part of me wants to sit here until sunrise, until this image is emblazoned so deep in my head that fifty years from now I'll be jerking my geriatric dick off to the memory.

"You have no idea what you do to me, do you?" My voice is full of awe.

"Probably the same thing every other woman you sleep with does to you. They make you cum," she says dryly, but I catch a hint of something else in her voice.

"No." I can't stand the thought of her thinking she's like Lulu or Raina or any one of the other women I've fucked. "You just don't get it, do you?"

"No, actually I don't, Gabriel. Help me understand," she whispers, and when I look down at her, the sleepiness has been replaced with something else. Something vulnerable. "You can have anyone you want. Why are you so insistent on having me?"

"I ..." My words trail off. How do I explain myself when I don't understand what's going on here myself?

The only way I know how, I guess. I'll show her.

I position myself on top of her, caging her head between my forearms, fitting my pelvis between her hips, pushing her thighs apart as far as they can go. I can't remember the last time I fucked a woman missionary style—normally I'm bending them over so I can close my eyes, get in deep and rough, and avoid kissing them—and yet this'll be twice now that I'm on top of Mercy, staring down into her eyes, anxious to see her face pinched with ecstasy.

"Look at me," I order, gently settling my forehead against hers until our eyelashes are fluttering against each other's and the brown of her irises is blurred. I roll my hips until the tip of my cock feels the warmth of her center, that wet spot that leads straight into heaven.

But unlike yesterday in the garage, I don't shove into her with one hard thrust. I barely move my hips this time, allowing myself to inch in slowly, all while our bodies are flush, her pert nipples pressed against mine, our faces nose to nose, our ragged breaths mixing together between us.

It's all I can do to keep from crying out.

"That *does* feel good," she rasps, her plump lips parting as her inner walls hug me tightly, as she stares up at me with unbridled lust, her fingers weaving through my hair, her thighs squeezing my hips. "You're not wearing a condom, are you?"

"I told you I wasn't going to." When I'm all the way in, I pause and take the opportunity to slip my tongue in to taste her mouth. Even after sleep, she tastes sweet. "You are the sexiest woman alive," I whisper, pulling out almost all the way, welcoming the ache of absence for a second or two before I slowly push back in.

She lets out a deep, guttural cry, and I nearly cum on the spot.

Fast and hard is not what I'm craving with her right now though. I can't handle it. Being inside her skin-to-skin is the best thing I've ever felt in my life.

I begin to roll my hips, reveling in her warmth, the feel of her naked flesh pressed against mine, the taste of her mouth, the graze of her nose as we grind. This is a thousand times more intimate than anything I've ever experienced with a woman before.

She drags her nails against my skin, her eyes remaining glued on mine as our bodies move together, as I pull out and push in, forcing myself to keep the rhythm painfully slow and steady.

"Your heart is beating so fast," she whispers breathlessly.

"So is yours." It's hammering against my chest, the plush mounds of her breasts unable to mask it. I graze my lips against hers and she responds eagerly, turning it into a kiss that I deepen instantly, our mouths moving against each other in the tantalizing dance of two people who can't get enough of each other.

I definitely can't get enough of Mercy.

And my balls are ready to burst despite the leisurely pace.

"Gabriel." My name is a moan on her lips. She pulls her legs up, spreading her thighs wider. Her hands roam my shoulders, my arms, my back. "I need to cum."

As badly as I want to do just that this very moment, I'm enjoying this sweet side of her too much to rush things. "Ask me nicely," I whisper, dragging the tip of my tongue over her lips.

Her eyelashes flutter as she peers up at me. "Please make me cum."

I roll my hips once in a circle, earning her gasp. "How badly do you need it?"

Her fingers dig into my ass, squeezing almost to the point of pain, and she jerks me forward, pulling me deeper into her. "I'm begging you."

Jesus Christ.

I begin thrusting my hips harder, faster, and not ten

seconds later I'm yelling as I shoot streams of cum deep inside her, marking her in a way I've never done to another woman before. She cries out, her own release making her tremble beneath me and pulse around me, her inner muscles draining me of every last drop.

"That was ..." Her words fade with her pants. She brushes the damp strands of my hair off my forehead and stares up at me with a mixture of bliss, awe, and confusion on her face. What's going on in her mind right now? Did she feel what I felt? That connection?

She swallows hard. "That wasn't dirty."

"No, it wasn't." I chuckle. "Don't worry, next time I'll make it extra dirty, sweetheart, I promise." She's so sexy-cute right now, I can't help but lean forward to steal one more slow, deep kiss. As much as I could just live in her all damn day, she should probably get a few more hours sleep. I slide my spent dick out of her heavenly wet spot and tuck in beside her.

I drift off more content than I remember being ... ever.

NINE
MERCY

If there is one thing that is predictable about this arrangement, it's that when my alarm goes off at 6:00 a.m., Gabriel won't stir. Though he fell asleep with his arms around me, I find him in his usual position on his side—hugging his pillow, the bedsheet sitting provocatively low on his perfect, shapely ass, his beautiful face boyish in sleep, his breathing shallow.

I wish he would stir.

I feel the overwhelming urge to wake him the way he woke me only hours ago, with my naked body pressed against his. I'm not complaining though. That was the most intimate, most incredible sex I've ever experienced.

And I can't begin to understand where it came from.

Gabriel isn't capable of something so personal, so emotional, is he? But it was him on top of me at 3:00 a.m., him slowly rolling his hips, devouring my mouth, keeping the pace slow, like he never wanted the moment to end. It felt like ... making love.

And when we finished climaxing, he gazed down at me and the look in his eyes was one of complete adoration.

Whoever that version of him was, I want him to come back again because I'm craving round two. But if I roll over and kiss him awake now, if I slide my hand down between the mattress and his body and stroke him awake, which version will I get? He did promise it dirty the next time, so will he fuck me raw?

Maybe the rougher version of him is safer, only because it's one hundred percent physical and less confusing for me.

Easing out of bed, I tiptoe to the bathroom. The insides of my thighs are still sticky from where he came inside me. Or maybe it was from me, from how wet I became the second I remembered that he wasn't wearing a condom, that we were skin to skin My body reacted as if it was aching for it, something that's never turned me on before.

But everything about Gabriel turns me on.

Even his semen.

His clothes are in a heap where he shed them last night. The soft gray T-shirt is hanging halfway in the trash. Did that land there in error?

I fish it out, noting the stains splattering the front of it. Brownish-red stains.

Bloodstains.

So many bloodstains.

Oh my God. I toss it back into the trash like it's on fire and dart to the sink to wash my hands, my own blood now rushing into my ears as I process this. Gabriel's face is fine. It's perfect. There's not a scratch.

So that must be someone else's blood.

Gabriel alluded to him going somewhere I wouldn't want to know about last night. What the hell was he doing? And where is this person who bled all over him now?

Are they alive? Did Gabriel hit them? Is that how he

ended up covered in someone else's blood? He'd have to hit the person repeatedly to produce that much of it.

So then what? He beat the hell out of someone—or worse—and then came back to have slow, sweet sex with me?

"Don't ask, don't tell, don't ask, don't tell, don't ask, don't tell …," I repeat over and over in a rushed whisper, scrubbing my hands clean of all evidence of whatever crime he was a part of while my stomach roils and my disappointment swells.

I remind myself yet again that no matter how incredible last night was, no matter how good he made me feel, Gabriel is still just a criminal who's found a way to get what he wants from me.

I quickly get ready for work and duck out without making a sound. For once, thankfully, Caleb isn't in the kitchen, allowing me to escape without having to deal with anyone in this godforsaken house.

Empire is already teeming with people when we pull into the valet line almost an hour later than I told Gabriel we'd be here.

"I could totally get used to this life." Michelle's eyes are sparkling as I ease the SUV forward. Ahead of us is a cobalt blue Porsche, transporting a silver fox in a suit and a leggy blond a third his age.

"What are you talking about? Your family owns a jewelry store in Scottsdale. You are used to this life." The Banks family lives on a multimillion-dollar ranch outside the city. Michelle has been trading in car keys to luxury sports cars every year since she was sixteen. Her downtown condo was bought and paid for with a trust fund. Her closet is the size of my shitty apartment bedroom, and it's full of expensive clothing, including the silky red dress I borrowed for tonight when I headed over there after my volunteer session to get ready for Gabriel's mandated night at Empire.

It's excessively short and looks more like a negligee than something you should leave your house in, and Michelle's eyes bugged out of her head when I chose it.

I'm not entirely sure why I did. A part of me wanted to rebel against Gabriel and not show up tonight. Clearly, I've been secretly hoping to discover that Gabriel is someone else—someone good, someone I can fall for—and after this morning, I know without a doubt that he is not that man. I just have to accept that. I have to give him what he wants and remind myself that I have an account full of money to pay for the best lawyer in the state.

And yet all I've been able to think about all day long is the bloody art print all over Gabriel's T-shirt and the utter distress that brings me.

I told him I don't want to know about his "activities," but right now, all I want to know is what happened last night. Where was he? Who was he with? Is someone dead?

The brake lights of the Porsche flash and then a valet is driving the car away. "What am I supposed to do?" Michelle may be of this world, but I'm still trying to get used to the navigation system on this thing.

"Just pull up and they'll take it from there. See? They're already ready for you," Michelle waves a freshly polished hand ahead, toward a skinny valet standing by. Two brawny bouncers step in behind him.

I do as told, and one of the bouncers—a sexy man with bright blue eyes and a clean-shaven head—opens my door before I'm even in park. "Good evening, Miss Wheeler. My name is Wayne. Please follow me," he croons in a deep baritone, offering a beefy arm. He's built like a linebacker, the seams of his suit looking one Hulk-flex away from ripping apart.

I guess Gabriel told them to expect us.

Gabriel texted me three times in the past hour, but I never responded to the messages. It's not the first time I've ignored him. I ignored him once before, after the Ambien night. I barely knew him then, and now I still barely know him but it's amazing how orgasming spectacularly with a man several times can fool you into believing you're somehow closer to him.

I wonder how he'll take my ignoring him now.

I guess I'm going to find out.

Michelle gets the same treatment on the other side with this bouncer's doppelgänger—only slightly smaller—and we're escorted past the long line of people waiting patiently in hopes of getting into the extravagant club.

"We have a table for you in VIP, but Mr. Easton would like to see you in his office first," Wayne announces, his booming voice carrying over the thrum of heady music. "Dwayne will escort your guest there now to wait for you."

"You're kidding me," I blurt out. "Wayne and Dwayne?"

He shrugs. I'm sure he's heard it a thousand times before.

I glance over with questioning eyes at Michelle, who's hanging off Dwayne, her tiny frame almost comical next to his.

"Go on. I'm fine." She waves me away. "I have company until you come back. Right?"

Dwayne flashes a crooked smile at her.

With that, I'm being led through the crowd like some

highly guarded celebrity by Wayne and two others who join us along the way, people parting to make way for the massive men. We round a corner and find two more looming bouncers, one who uses his radio to report in to someone. He gestures up the steep flight of steps to where another brawny bouncer stands beside a heavy, black metal door. "Mr. Easton's waiting for you."

"Thanks." I don't remember there being this much security when Gabriel was leading me through the kitchen to the back alley. Is this even normal for a club? Or is this just the kind of security you need when you're part of the Easton crime family?

I ponder this as I carefully climb the steps in Michelle's four-inch, red heels, my hand tucked behind me in hopes of not flashing the four men standing below, should they be watching. I fight the urge to turn around to see if they are. Meanwhile, with each step closer to that heavy, black door ahead, the flutters in my stomach grow more rampant.

The man at the top of the stairs opens the door for me.

"Thanks," I offer with a polite smile. His stony face doesn't so much as twitch.

Okay then. I duck into the office and quickly survey my surroundings. It looks more like an extension of the club—a lounge, with dark walls, leather couches, and a small alcove with shelves of liquor. One wall is all glass and it overlooks the club's dance floor. Muted flashes of purple and blue stream in as the vibrant lightshow plays in time with the DJ.

The only element in here that screams office is a desk, and it's currently occupied by an enormous man with a clean-shaven head, dressed all in black, his polished shoes propped atop its surface.

I quickly skip over him though, unable to keep my appreciative gaze off the man standing across from me, casually leaning against a pillar, his brawny arms crossed over his chest. Gabriel is wearing a pewter dress shirt tonight that brings out the steely blue in his eyes. His black pants fit his muscular thighs. A part of me wants to ask him to turn around so I can appreciate the way they hug his firm ass. His hair is full and styled perfectly, his jaw is freshly shaven, his lips plump and slightly parted, waiting to be kissed.

Gabriel's gaze drags over me, and I can feel his eyes like fingertips tracing my collarbone, flicking at my nipples, dipping into my bellybutton, slipping beneath the short hem of my dress to tease the apex of my thighs. My body betrays me, flushing with eagerness despite the dark worrisome thoughts still swirling in my head about what he has done.

He doesn't stop his appraisal until he reaches my stilettos, and when his eyes lift again ...

They're as dark and stormy as they were that first day in Fulcort's visitor room.

A predator's gaze.

My stomach drops.

"And on that note ..." The man behind the desk stands, allowing me to appreciate the full size of him. He must be six foot five, at least. "It's ten to eleven," He says to Gabriel. A warning.

"I know what time it is," Gabriel replies smoothly, his gaze never breaking from mine.

Oh shit.

Well, he's pissed.

I guess that means sex won't be sweet this time around.

The idea of that shouldn't thrill me as much it does. What has Gabriel turned me into?

The man smirks as he passes by me, smoothing a hand

over his shirt as his eyes roll over my dress. He didn't even bother to introduce himself, which irritates me. Does he think I'm just another one of Gabriel's women? Here today, gone tomorrow?

"Tell Marcus to knock when they get here, but don't disturb us for any other reason," Gabriel warns in a sharp tone. "I don't care if the club is burning down."

The man strolls out the door. It sounds like a heavy vault door when it shuts, leaving us alone with nothing but the muted thrum of bass pounding through the walls and my heart pounding in my chest.

"You summoned me?" I say in a forced calm voice, folding my arms over my chest, mainly to hide the fact that my nipples are probably erect enough to cut glass.

"What took you so long to get here? I was expecting you an hour ago," he asks in an overly calm, cool tone.

"It takes time to look this good," I counter, doing a sweeping motion with my hands over my dress.

His gaze trails it, flaring with heat. "So much time that you couldn't respond to a single message from me?"

Yeah, he really doesn't like his texts being ignored. "You asked me to meet you here tonight. Well, here I am. But I'm not your girlfriend, Gabriel. So let's not pretend."

"And yet you are mine for the next month." Gabriel stalks toward me like a cheetah moving in on its prey, the intention in his gaze unmistakable. "Or have you forgotten?"

"How could I possibly forget? You remind me every chance you get," I snap. I wonder if I'm a fool for not being more afraid of him,.of what he could do to me.

He reaches up to toy with a strand of my jet-black hair, curled with Michelle's broad iron to give me sexy, beachy waves. There is a perplexed look on his face. "Last night was ..." His words drift with a hard swallow. "I thought you enjoyed it. Did something happen to change that?" I could be wrong, but I think I catch a hint of apprehension in his voice.

You tell me what happened last night, Gabriel.

I swallow. "You're paying me to fuck you. What else do you want?"

"Your heart," he blurts out and then frowns, as if he just surprised himself. But he doesn't backpedal. He doesn't say anything. He simply stares at me.

I'm a fish out of water for a few moments, my mouth gaping open and shut. "I already told you that you can't have it. I'll never give that to you." That would amount to emotional suicide. "Besides, you don't want my heart. You just hate that there's something you can't buy."

"That's not—" He cuts himself off, a glower taking over his face. He checks his watch.

"You have someone coming soon. I'll go downstairs. Michelle's waiting for me anyway."

"No. Not yet." His jaw tenses as he strolls over to the door to drop a metal lever down, locking the door. Then he takes a seat behind the desk. "Come here." More than anything, he sounds tired.

Cautiously, I do as asked, stopping in front of him.

His gaze settles on my thighs. There is no mistaking the bulge in his pants. "Turn around and lean over the desk," he orders softly.

My stomach flips with excitement as I do as asked, resting my forearms against the smooth surface. The position forces my dress up to uncover the skimpy red lace panties I chose for underneath.

Gabriel doesn't disappoint with his reaction, inhaling sharply. He has prime view from behind, after all. His calloused hands smooth over each cheek and then his fingertips hook under the elastic band of my panties. He pulls them down, off my hips, and lets them fall to the floor.

My body reacts instantly, heat beginning to pool at the apex of my thighs.

"Won't give me your heart," he murmurs, dragging one finger through my slick folds, making my sex clench in response, "but the rest of you seems happy to have me here."

"It's all I can trust you with," I admit without thinking. It's true. Gabriel is a god with my body. I can hand over control of my physical pleasure. But my heart?

The only thing I could trust is that in the end he'd shred that to pieces.

I hold my breath and I wait for him to do something. Anything.

A word, a touch, a kiss. I wait for the sound of his zipper unfastening.

I wait for what feels like forever. My assets are on full display at eye level to Gabriel. Not that they haven't been before, but these office lights are harsh.

And then the desk drawer rolls open. I glance over in time to see Gabriel fish out a small bottle of lube.

My nervousness spikes. "What's that for?"

"I promised you extra dirty this time around, didn't I?" His hands are on my thighs, pushing them farther part.

I'm intrigued. But ... "Don't you have a meeting is in ten minutes?"

"This won't take long. Arch your back."

I do as asked, equal parts curious and mortified at my exposure.

The sound of him squeezing the bottle comes a second before a glob of cool, slippery liquid hits my backside. I bite my lip to stifle my gasp at the sensation.

"I'm going to have this one day soon," Gabriel drags his finger through the lube, smearing it around my tight entrance, drawing circles, pushing until the ring of muscle gives and his finger slips in. "But not tonight.."

My inner muscles clench at the idea of something of that size in there. I'm not sure if that appeals to me or not, but I do trust Gabriel.

He's rifling around in the drawer again, and a moment later his finger is slipping out of me and something hard is replacing it.

"What is that?" I ask warily as he drizzles more lube.

"You've never used one of these before?"

"No." I've never used toys of any kind with a man before, but I don't admit that now.

He draws tiny circles with the smooth end, teasing me. "It's a plug. You're going to wear it for me until we get home."

My eyes widen. "You want me to walk around the club with something in my ass? Are you out of your mind?" And why the hell does he have one of those in his office desk!

"Whenever ... whatever ...," he murmurs softly, echoing the terms of our arrangement. He adds pressure to the circular ministrations and my tight entrance gives way, accepting the smooth metal. There's a slight burn with the stretch and there's no missing the fact that it's there—inside me—but otherwise it's not horrible.

"There, you're good." He smooths a palm over my cheek affectionately. "Stand."

I do, the hem of my dress slipping down. Yes, I can definitely feel it inside me.

Gabriel leans over to collect my panties, holding them out. I gingerly slip my feet through and he eases them up and back in place. "See? Not so bad. Especially if you decide to hit the dance floor."

"And you know this how?"

He shrugs. "Or so I've heard."

I flash a wicked grin. "How about you bend over for me so you can learn firsthand?"

He fixes the hem of my dress, his lip curled at the corner. "Something tells me you wouldn't even have the decency to use lube on me."

I can't help my bark of laughter. "You're right, you are smart." I eye my reflection in the wall of windows. "That's one-way, right?" Because if anyone saw Gabriel inserting a plug into my ass, I will die of mortification.

He leans back in the chair, his legs splayed, his erection taunting me through his pants. "Of course. Do you think we'd want anyone seeing the kinds of things that go on in our private office?"

"Are you referring to your staff orgies or making someone bleed all over your clothes?" It's a bitter accusation that just slips out, unbidden, and in that moment I realize just how upset—how not okay—I am with Gabriel being who he is.

How much I was hoping he was someone different.

"What are you ..." Gabriel frowns, and a moment later recognition passes over his face. "You went through my trash."

"I thought it might have accidentally landed there, so I pulled it out and ... yeah."

"It didn't accidentally land there." He says it so simply.

I know I shouldn't ask, but I do anyway. "Whose blood was that, Gabriel?" My voice is shaky. "What were you doing last night?"

He hesitates. "I thought you didn't want me to lie to you?"

"Jesus Christ." Suddenly I feel light-headed. I maneuver away from him, needing space. Each step reminds me that there's a foreign object inside me.

"It's not what you think," he begins.

"Yeah, whatever," I mutter, making my way to the panel of windows. I study the horde of writhing bodies on the dance floor. It's impossible to see Michelle in the VIP section from here, but I'm sure she's there, lapping up the special treatment on account of her best friend being a sex slave to one of the owners.

The office chair squeaks, and I catch Gabriel's reflection in the window, approaching me. "Is this why you're acting the way you are?"

"How am I acting?"

He sidles up behind me and rests his hands on my hips. I can feel their warmth through the delicate fabric of my dress. "Like I'm some asshole propositioning you in the prison parking lot. Like you hate my guts again." He leans in to lay a slow kiss just below my ear. "Like last night didn't mean anything to you."

I grit my teeth. "I don't hate you anymore." Maybe that's the problem. It was easier to dismiss who Gabriel was before, when I despised him. While I don't exactly know what I feel for him, I know it's not hatred. Every time I give myself to him physically, he manages to steal a little something else.

"Last night wasn't what you're thinking, Mercy."

I dare turn to meet his eyes. "Then what was it?"

He watches the gyrating bodies on the dance floor for a long moment, his jaw taut as if fighting the urge to speak. "I was at an underground fighting ring," he finally admits. "And it got ugly."

"You were fighting last night?" I frown as I search his beautiful face, grab his hands to check his knuckles. Nothing.

He chuckles. "Not me. One of our fighters. That was his blood all over me. He got hurt pretty bad and I was helping him out."

"You have fighters? Like boxing?"

He shrugs. "Sort of."

Someone bangs on the door.

Gabriel sighs heavily. "Look, I shouldn't be telling you this, but believe me when I say, I didn't hurt anyone last night and no one was forced into anything. It's all for money. A lot of money."

"The illegal kind?"

"The kind that buys all kinds of things." He twists his lips. "Like protection for people in prison."

Like the protection Gabriel offered my father.

It begins to sink in. Gabriel didn't hurt anyone last night. He didn't kill anyone.

My knees threaten to buckle with the overwhelming relief I'm feeling right now.

He collects my chin between his thumb and forefinger to pull my face to his. His gaze pierces me with its intensity. "Listen to me very carefully, Mercy: you can never talk about this with anyone. Not your blond friend down there, not your therapist, not your dad. No one. Understood? As far as anyone knows, you know nothing."

Because if I know something that could put Gabriel—and whoever he's involved with—behind bars, then I become a liability. And liabilities get disappeared. That's how it works with these things, isn't it?

Or is that just on TV?

I nod dumbly. I'm just so happy it's not what I thought it was.

"Okay." His fingers gently brush strands of my hair, as if afraid to disturb the styled waves. He smiles at me. "I have to deal with these guys now but after, I'll come find you and we can pick up where we left off." He leans in to drag his tongue over my lips. "You're going to like this, I promise."

Furious pounding rattles the door.

"Fucking Caleb," he mutters. Letting go of me, he strolls over to release the lock.

A moment later, the office door flies open and the older Easton brother marches in, a glower marring his normally handsome face. "Seriously? You made me stand out there like a chump while you're in here chasing pussy?" he barks, his hostile tone so foreign to his normally relaxed "nothing bothers me" drawl. I note the angry cut across his bottom lip. The result of a hard punch is my guess.

He likely deserved it.

"Chill," Gabriel says calmly. "You're too wound up."

"Mercy. Out. Now," Caleb barks, punctuating it with a thumb jerk toward the door.

"What the fuck!" Gabriel roars, his calm demeanor evaporating as he rounds the desk, charging toward his brother. "Don't you ever talk to her like—"

"You want Camillo Perri hearing about her? Huh?" Caleb's eyebrows arch. "You want him knowing you have someone? How well did that turn out for Mom?"

Uh ... what?

"Jesus Christ," Gabriel snaps. "It's not the same."

"Bullshit it's not, Gabe. Bullshit." The two Easton men stand chest to chest, glaring at each other, tension swirling.

And I'm just the innocent bystander, wondering what the hell is going on.

"Mike just radioed to say they've pulled in," Caleb says in a more even tone. "He'll be leading them up here in a few minutes, and you really don't want them knowing what I know. What you're too stubborn to admit to, yet." Caleb gives him a high-browed look.

Gabriel's jaw tenses, his eyes flashing to me.

"Seriously, if this alliance goes south—"

"Okay! Shut the fuck up already." Gabriel's arm is out before he even reaches me, ready to herd me out the door. "Michelle is likely wondering where you are."

Michelle has likely already found another toy for the night, if Dwayne the bouncer didn't take the bait she was so freely casting out.

"Is your friend hot?" Caleb calls out, as if that verbal spat between him and Gabriel didn't just happen.

"Too hot for you," I retort, annoyed with the way he dismissed me so callously. But maybe he has good reason. Maybe his intentions are good.

"Is that so ...?" Caleb's lips curl, and some semblance of the version I know—not the scary one that just stormed in here—appears. "That sounds like a challenge."

I'm about to tell him to not bother when I'm distracted by Gabriel's hand settling on my ass, his palm subtly pressing against the round base that anchors this damn thing in place.

"I'll meet you down there as soon as I can. Order whatever you two want, it's on Empire." He leans in to settle an affectionate kiss on my temple. It's his dismissal.

I hesitate, Caleb's words from the other day about Gabriel getting them into trouble coming to the forefront. That coupled with Caleb's demeanor and words like "alliance" and "goes south" makes me wonder if something bad is about to go down in this office? Whoever this Camillo Perri guy is, I'm guessing he's dangerous. "Be careful." It sounds like the right thing to say.

He gives me his signature arrogant smirk, the one that says he's not afraid of anything or anyone. I wonder if that's actually true, though. "Careful on these stairs. They're steep, and those shoes of yours are high."

I'm hit with a blast of pumping music the moment I step out. Their office must be soundproofed. I pick my way down the steep stairs on account of my stilettos and the plug, my teeth gritting against the odd sensation walking stirs. He's right, I don't hate it. I don't know that I love it, but what I do love is another round of sex with Gabriel later.

Wayne meets me at the bottom, his appreciative gaze on my thighs, though he has the decency to avert his eyes when I catch him staring.

"This way to Miss Banks," his deep voice booms as he holds a hand out, prompting me to move ahead and to the left.

We're about halfway to the VIP section when the kitchen doors swing open and two sharply dressed men step out, flanked by men on both sides. Men who don't look like bouncers but who definitely look like protection.

The moment I lay eyes on them, I know these are the guys meeting with Gabriel and Caleb. I slow to study them and gather as much information as I can. They're young, I note. Late twenties, early thirties, like Gabriel and Caleb. Young and attractive. And likely related, because they bear a striking resemblance to each other, though one has medium brown hair and a beard, while the more slender one ahead of him has dark blond hair and a more chiseled face.

The blond guy's eyes are roving the club. They pass me and keep going, barely stalling. But I catch the eye of the bearded one, locking gazes by accident. He has baby blue eyes.

Soft eyes.

Gentle eyes.

Is that the Camillo Perri that Caleb didn't want me around for?

He holds my attention, taking in my dress, his gaze flickering behind me to Wayne before landing on me again, the corners of his mouth curling up a touch as if he knows a secret.

We pass and, as hard as it is, I resist the urge to turn back and steal another glance. I continue on toward the VIP section.

"Third booth in. Gabe said it's your favorite," Wayne says, gesturing to the table where Michelle sits, twirling an olive stick in her dirty martini, batting eyelashes at Dwayne.

Of course he said that. It's the table Gabriel fucked me on. Thank God for the dim lights to hide my blush.

A busty blond with a tiny, black tube top and Band-Aid skirt appears out of the shadows, holding a tray with empty glasses. "Something to drink?" she asks, with a smile that doesn't reach her blue eyes. Her hair is slicked back in a ponytail, not a hair amiss. It's a severe look that accentuates her high cheekbones.

Gabriel did say to order whatever we wanted, but I'm too overwhelmed to think. I nod toward Michelle, casting a dismissive wave. "Whatever she's having."

"Merce!" Michelle waves, giving me her "I'm drunk" grin.

I slide in gingerly, feeling the plug move inside me, the

pressure from sitting in the booth equal parts uncomfortable and erotic.

"Are you okay?" She frowns. "You're moving like you hurt."

Hurt would definitely not be the right word for what I'm feeling right now. "Just trying not to flash anyone in this short dress," I lie. "I'm sorry I left you out here so long. We had to go over a few things." Like how Gabriel is involved in an underground fighting ring. All things considered, that's not so bad.

Another wave of relief swarms me. For the first time since this morning, I allow myself to look back on last night through my rose-colored glasses again.

"No worries. I've had Dwayne to keep me company. He's staying by our table all night to keep the creeps away." She gives me wide, knowing eyes. "So I guess I'll just have to hit on him."

TEN
GABRIEL

"Are you cool, Caleb?"

"Yeah, yeah," he mutters dismissively.

"Really? Then why are you pacing like a caged lion?" Back and forth in front of the panel of windows, his gaze hard and far away, looking ready to pounce at the first opportunity.

He pauses midstep, as if only realizing what he's doing now that I've called him on it. With a deep breath, he heads to the wet bar to pour himself a vodka.

Jesus Christ. I can't remember the last time I saw Caleb frazzled. This doesn't bode well for this meeting, and the Perris haven't even made it up the goddamn stairs yet. "No repeats of what happened with Vic, huh?" I warn him. From what Detective Stan dug up on Merrick and Vince, my guess is that neither of these guys would be as easy to subdue as our cousin, despite their sparkling, baby blue eyes.

The two of them are a lot like us, enjoying what life has to offer with fast cars and party weekends. Expect of course for those few years Vince spent in a state pen in his early twenties for a weapons charge—he got off on the violent assault that would have seen him locked up for another decade. And Merrick may be younger and leaner, but he's been heavily into MMA fighting since he was twelve. He also likes dick as much as, if not more than, pussy, a fact that seems to be under wraps on account of Camillo Perri being a homophobic asshole. According to Stan, Daddy has no idea.

I don't know what's more shocking to me—that Camillo hasn't heard through the grapevine or how the fuck Stan finds this shit out.

Caleb's tongue darts out to test the cut he earned from our cousin for his efforts. "There's no pool here. And, hey, I've shown restraint before."

"Oh, you're right," I say with mock appeasement. That time we caught a guy in here, trying to crack the Winchester in the wall? Caleb was angling to launch him through the window. I reminded him what a corpse on a crowded dance floor would do for business, and he held back.

He broke both his arms and then threw him down the stairs instead.

I sigh. "Pour me one of those, will ya? And maybe bring a few empty glasses over here, for our guests." They did agree to fly here again with only a day's notice, after all.

"Can't wait until this is over." Caleb dumps several crystal tumblers on the edge of the desk.

"Me, too." Because the sooner we're done here, the sooner I can get back to Mercy. I should have known she'd see the T-shirt this morning. I honestly didn't think anything of it. But if I had hidden it, we wouldn't have had this tension. And I wouldn't have felt compelled to tell her about the illegal fighting ring with the prison in order to explain myself. The very thing I told Caleb I'd never do. He'll lose it if he finds out. It was stupid on my part—it puts her in danger if she were to talk—and yet I couldn't keep it from her. I needed her to stop looking at me the way she was when she walked through that door, a siren in a red dress with ice in her eyes.

I wanted her to look at me like she did last night.

Fucking Caleb called it—I'm falling hard for this woman, and I can't stand the idea that she doesn't feel the same way about me. Won't feel the same way about me.

I need to find a way to win her over.

I can do it, I promise myself. Look how far we've come, from her glaring at me like she's sizing up where to slit my throat for most impact, to having no qualms about bending over my desk when I ask her to.

I just have to prove to her that I'm not as bad as she thinks I am.

And that I can change.

A loud knock sounds on the door.

My brother and I share a look.

"You set?" He nods toward the desk where the Glock is loaded and ready, should the need arise. Not that it will. The Perri brothers were thoroughly searched for weapons and wires, and we've already done a sweep for bugs in here.

"All good."

Caleb strolls over and opens the door.

I've had the pleasure of seeing Merrick and Vince recently, but this is a first for Caleb in years. He edges back, studying the two men at length as they saunter in.

Vince offers his hand, as I expected him to. He seems to be the one to always take the lead.

Caleb eyes Vince's hand a moment, but then accepts it.

Merrick follows suit. "It's been a while."

At least twelve years, if I remember correctly. A weekend in Vegas, with fake IDs and a suite at the Bellagio crawling with high-priced escorts. We ran into these two at the blackjack table. Didn't realize who they were at first, but once we figured it out, Caleb had Vince in a chokehold that security had to break apart.

I nod toward Dylan, and he pulls the door shut, locking the four of us in.

For a moment, we simply stand there, staring at each other. Probably all wondering the same thing—how the fuck did it come to this? That my father suggested the meeting is a bad omen for things to come, though he has no idea what this meeting is really about. What does Camillo Perri think about an alliance though?

"Does your father know we're meeting?" Caleb asks. He must be thinking along the same lines as me.

"He knows we're meeting to discuss the problem of the cartel. He agrees that a temporary alliance would be beneficial. That's what we told Leo and Miles, too." Vince's lips quirk. "That's all they know."

"And that's all they'd suspect," Merrick adds.

"Well, to be fair, your brothers don't seem to be too sharp, given other key details about their family members that they've missed." Caleb locks a knowing gaze with Merrick.

The youngest Perri son rolls his shoulders and adjusts his stance, his blue eyes turning cold with a silent challenge, a "say something out loud, asshole" dare. The thing is, if they've done any research on us—which I'm sure they have —they'd know that Caleb is an "anything goes" kind of guy when it comes to sexual proclivities.

But what the hell, does he always have to push buttons?

"This is quite the club you have," Vince says in a loud

voice, as if to distract from the brewing explosion. "I told Gabe when we paid a visit last weekend that we're envious. It's something Merrick and I have talked about getting into, but we wouldn't know where to start."

"We didn't, either. We found the right people to help us get on our feet," I say, to keep the conversation going.

"And the clientele ..." Vince whistles. "After we're done here, I have someone I need to track down." He nods toward the windows and the dance floor beyond.

"The red dress," Merrick says absently, a smirk curling his lips. "You looked ready to trail her like a lost puppy."

"I'm going to follow that woman right into her fucking bed, tonight, is what I'm gonna do," Vince says, lust in his eyes.

There's no way they're not talking about Mercy.

"She's off-limits," I warn through clenched teeth, struggling to keep my calm. "Don't even look at her."

Vince's eyes narrow with calculation, as if he's sizing up my instant reaction. Finally, he shrugs. "Not my fault, with the way she was checking me out."

"She's not interested in you," I snap. *Is she?*

Now it's Caleb's turn to clear his throat and give me a warning look.

I grit out a smile and gesture at the leather chairs we pulled up to our desk ahead of their entrance. "Please, take a seat."

The brothers share a wary look, Merrick deferring to his older brother.

In the end, they both move in together, but cautiously.

They don't know what to make of us, either, it seems.

Caleb folds his arms over his chest, remaining standing over them. "So tell us ... what made you ever think that

Gabe and I would need your help against our father?" Right to the point.

"We weren't completely sure," Merrick admits, his eyes skittering over my brother's solid frame, stalling just below his belt.

I stifle my smile. Caleb is the kind of guy to try anything once, but I think he might draw the line at letting the Eastons' arch enemy suck his dick. Or maybe not. He is also the kind of guy to send a close-up video of the act to Camillo.

"But with what your cousin has been saying lately—" Vince begins.

"What has Vic been saying?" Caleb cuts in, his jaw clenching. It could only be Vic. Alexei isn't stupid enough to shoot off his mouth loud enough for the Perris to hear.

The brothers share another look, as if deciding who wants to share.

"That Vlad Easton hasn't figured out he's basically a breathing corpse, and his sons are too weak to take over for him," Merrick says smoothly.

Even the faint thrum of music from the club can't drown out the sound of Caleb's teeth gnashing.

"We know you're not. Weak, I mean," Vince jumps in. "We've heard enough stories to know you two get shit done. So we figured, if you two haven't stepped in yet, maybe it's because you're like us and you want to branch out into other things, away from anything that'll guarantee you a cell for life."

"Our father and two older brothers have been pressuring us to get more involved with the family business for years. If Vlad is anything like our father ..." Merrick's lips twist with bitterness.

"Family ... loyalty ...," I mock, taking a sip of vodka.

"Respect," Vince booms in a deep mock-Italian accent, earning his brother's smirk.

"So, what are you two proposing?" Caleb asks, his layer of suspicion still firmly in place.

"Well, first things first." Vince reaches into his shirt pocket and pulls out a folded piece of paper. "Here is a peace offering. Or a token of trust." He frowns. "I don't know what the fuck you want to call it, but, anyway, here it is." He tosses the paper on the desk.

I steal a glance at my brother before reaching for it.

It's a photograph of that weasel son-of-a-whore third cousin of ours, the one who ratted out my father, sitting in the front passenger seat of a dark sedan in a parking lot. I recognize the man sitting behind the wheel as Special Agent Jim DeShaw, the Fed who led the surveillance charge on my father.

But there's someone tucked away in the back seat, too. I squint, trying to make out his face. "Is that ...?" It's dim, but his profile—the broad nose, the steep forehead, the brim of his fedora—is disturbingly familiar.

"Yup," Merrick confirms. "And check out the time stamp."

Holy shit. It was taken one day before the Feds kicked down our father's door and dragged him out of his house in his striped boxers and wife-beater.

Uncle Peter was meeting with the Feds.

I hand the photo to Caleb, who quickly scans it. "What the fuck is this?" he mutters, but I know he's already putting two and two together. "Who took this picture?" he demands.

Merrick offers him a casual shrug in response. "We have our guy. Just like you have your guy. You know, the one you had digging to find dirt on us." He matches my brother's knowing gaze.

"I don't believe this." Caleb tosses the pic the desk. "That doesn't make sense. Peter's the one who dealt with Marek." And this picture would mean that Uncle Peter was working with the rat. But there's no other explanation for why he'd be in that car with them. And the fact that Uncle Peter's not doing time alongside my dad means the Feds didn't have anything to hold over him, otherwise they would have forced him to testify, especially after Marek "disappeared." That means he was helping the Feds nail my father voluntarily.

We always did wonder how that lowlife cousin knew some of the things he knew. Times and dates and places we didn't remember telling him. And how Uncle Peter found out about Marek's betrayal before any of us did. He told us he had his internal sources, but why didn't he come to us with that information before acting? By the time DeHavilland caught wind of the FBI's informant who was willing to turn on our father, Marek was already eating lead, courtesy of our dear uncle, who told us he wasn't going to trust any of our hired guys to do it.

If this picture tells the right story, then Peter must have fed Marek just enough details to give to the FBI, who had just enough to put Dad away, and then he dispatched him. He wanted dad in prison for long enough that he likely wouldn't see freedom again. He wanted him out of the picture, but he didn't have the balls to off him.

Because then he'd have to deal with us.

As much as we both despise our father, this is a betrayal we can't let slide.

"You Eastons have an interesting way of interpreting loyalty." Merrick smirks.

I look at my brother and see that he's thinking along the same lines as I am.

Though shocking, this is all beginning to make sense. It also could be a trap.

"How do we know this isn't some huge setup to have us off each other and leave the path free and clear for you and your family?" Caleb's voice is thick with accusation. "After what you did to our mother—"

"*Your* family's hands aren't clean either," Vince reminds him with steely calm.

"Not on the same level, man." Caleb's face twists with disgust. "The fact that we're even sitting across a table from you right now makes me sick."

"Why should we trust you?" I ask, trying to rein this back in before it comes to blows. My gaze is focused on Merrick. He has the weaker poker face of the two.

He levels me with a hard gaze. "Because we aren't like the rest of our family." He swallows hard. "Your mother—" He clears his throat. "It was wrong, what they did to her."

"Do you even know what they did to her?" Caleb hisses. He looks ready to attack.

Merrick nods, his eyes downcast.

It's Vince who speaks. "We were there," he admits sullenly. "We saw the whole thing."

My stomach twists.

"I was twelve, Merrick was nine. Dad told us to get into the back seat of the Suburban and shut our mouths. We were too soft, according to him. We needed to be tough like Miles and Leo were at our age."

I don't know much about the two older Perris except that they're a lot older—in their early forties now—and apparently as conniving as their father. Miles, far more so.

Vince bites his lip. "There was a woman sitting in the

middle seat with a bag over her head. We didn't know who she was, but she was crying hard, begging them to let her go, that her husband would pay anything to have her back." His eyes flash to Caleb, who's pacing again, before darting to the polished floor. "They drove to an abandoned warehouse, pulled the woman out. Dad told us to watch. And we saw what they did to her."

Jesus Christ. What kind of father does that to his own sons? Even Vlad Easton wouldn't do that.

"We didn't know she was your mom until a few days later, when we saw the news," Merrick admits quietly.

"Does it matter who it was? She was an innocent woman!" Caleb booms.

"Cale ...," I warn.

"Our father is the one who pulled the trigger on her," Merrick says.

"And what about the other stuff. The stuff leading up to that?" I manage to ask, my throat burning.

Vince squeezes his eyes shut as if trying to rid that from his memories. "That was Miles. Leo and my father didn't lay a hand on her. They let it happen, but that was *all Miles*."

I see it coming a millisecond before it happens. Caleb winds back and launches his glass into the air. It flies straight for the window, slamming into it with a loud bang. Crystal explodes into countless shards all over the office, leaving a spiderweb of cracked glass. Miraculously though, the window holds.

"Caleb!" I'm on my feet and rushing to check the view of the dance floor below to see if we need to do damage control. A few curious heads have turned, people looking up. They must have heard it, being that close, but they likely can't see the damage. I sigh. "We need to get this taped up pronto." All that bass from the speakers is liable to make this shatter, and then we've got a problem.

While I'm here, I can't help but let my gaze wander. I spot the flash of crimson on the dance floor. Mercy's dancing with her blond friend. Wayne and Dwayne are solid pinnacles within easy reach, and the hounds circling seem aware. Oh, but no ... there's one dumb fuck, moving in to grind up behind Mercy.

My teeth clench. *Three ...two ...*

Wayne grabs the guy's shoulders with his meaty paws and yanks him backward, away from her.

I breathe a sigh of relief. Good thing, too, because if that had lasted any longer, he would be looking for a new job. I told him as much. No one is getting near my girl, especially when she's as volatile as she must be right now. Or so I've heard. Lulu and Raina spend half their shifts with plugs in their asses, for fun. By the time they come for Caleb or me, they're practically already orgasming.

I smile at the thought of Mercy anxiously waiting for me like that. When she walked in wearing that tiny, silky dress and those fuck-me shoes, it was all I could do not to take the few minutes I had and fuck her right over this desk.

"Why do you seem so adamant on throwing Miles under the bus?" Caleb demands, jabbing a finger in the air, his voice now icy calm. "After *all these years*, why show up here now and rip open painful wounds? Because you know I'm going to do something, right? I don't give a fuck about any sort of truce now that I know for certain that it was your brother. You're smart enough to know that, right?"

"I *am* smart enough." Merrick nods, studying his hands a moment. "And I'll be happy to see him get what he deserves."

"Why?" I ask before my brother has a chance, followed by realization. "You guys are afraid of him."

His jaw tenses. It's a few moments before he speaks again. "I was seeing someone not long ago." He hesitates, his gaze flashing to Caleb ever so smoothly. "His name was Ryan. We were keeping it quiet until we didn't have to."

"What would decide that?"

Vince sighs. "Our father is ill. It's terminal. He has maybe another year left."

"Nobody knows about it," Merrick adds.

"My fucking condolences," Caleb mutters with pure venom, before I have a chance to say something similar. I don't ask what he's ill with. I don't give a damn. I can only hope that getting pumped with opioids won't help that old snake, that he'll leave this world in constant, excruciating pain.

Whatever the diagnosis is, it must be buried deep if even Stan didn't ferret it out.

"We figured that once he was gone, we'd be free to go our separate ways. Live our lives the way we want to. But it seems Miles is more like our father than we realized." Merrick studies his hands a moment, and when he looks up again, I note the slight sheen over his eyes before he blinks it away. "Ryan disappeared about a month ago. I went over to his place and he was just gone. There'd definitely been a struggle. Things were broken. His wallet and phone were still there. I went home, ready to call our guy to track him down, and Miles was waiting for me there with the gold chain I'd given Ryan on his birthday." He presses his lips together a moment. "It was covered in blood. He said Ryan wouldn't be coming around any time ... ever."

Shit. Miles is next-generation Camillo. And possibly more evil.

Caleb sighs heavily and, without saying another word, pours vodkas into fresh glasses, handing one to the younger Perri first.

Merrick accepts it with an appreciative nod, and we all take a moment with our thoughts.

Caleb finally takes a seat. "So you don't hold any loyalty to your brother."

"Loyalty?" Merrick scoffs. "I want the fucker dead."

"But you don't have big enough balls to do it."

"My balls are just fine." Merrick's jaw tenses. "But he's my brother. How can I do that?"

"But you know *we* can. And will, given what you just told us." Caleb leans back in his chair with a smug smile as the pieces all fit together. He's impressed, I can tell.

"So, Camillo has one foot in the grave, Miles belongs in a grave, and Uncle Peter is going to be in a grave once we show our father this picture," I muse. That's a lot of holes to dig.

"It's all just a matter of the dominos falling the right way, at the right time," Vince agrees.

"But Camillo isn't going anywhere just yet. And we'd still have the problem of our father. With Uncle Peter out of the picture, he'll be pushing us even harder to run Harriet. He can't do it from inside." Caleb chugs the last of his vodka. He's going to be a wreck tonight. Then again, so am I, if I'm not careful. I toss back the last of my drink.

Vince frowns. "Harriet?"

"Don't fucking ask," Caleb mutters, shaking his head. "But, say for shits and giggles that our fathers are out of the picture somehow—"

"We can convince our father that taking out Miles was Vlad's doing. That he needs to go after him directly," Merrick suggests. "Your dad's a sitting duck in there."

Jesus. I rub my brow. Are we really talking about this? He *is* our father, however hateful he may be.

"Right. So that would leave Leo on your side, and Vic and Alexei on ours," Caleb says, continuing along on this dark path. "They're the only ones who'd fight to keep that business going, and they'd be happy to cut us out."

"Let them take on the cartel together then," Vince says. "Problem solved."

Caleb snorts through a sip of his drink. "Have fun with that."

This is actually happening. We're actually sitting around this desk, plotting murder. Multiple murders. The targets have earned their death certificates many times over, but still.

A nervous twinge stirs in my gut but I tamp it down. The world will be a better place without them. "So then ... we need a game plan." I look to each of them in turn. "We need to make nice and pretend that we're moving forward with the alliance they all think we're here talking about." Because if any of them caught wind of what was *really* going on, it would mean war.

"Yeah, no offense, but I don't trust that fucking uncle of yours not to stab us in the back," Merrick says with a pointed look.

"Something we finally agree on." Caleb lifts his glass, and the youngest Perri man clinks it.

"So then what are we going to do? We need a plan," I push. Ideally, one that smears as little blood on our hands as possible.

Caleb sighs and pours another round.

ELEVEN
MERCY

"Why did he make you come here if he's going to be somewhere else all night?" Michelle scoffs.

I shrug. "Because he can?"

"I guess it *could* be worse." Michelle waves a manicured hand around the VIP section—dark alcoves of private tables and pricey bottle service, for those so inclined—and then at the empty glass in her hand.

Dwayne notices and leans in. "You want another round?"

"Would you, my darling?" She grins up at him, her dangly earrings catching the light to sparkle.

His eyes twinkle with his chuckle. "Extra dirty this time?"

"*So* dirty." She winks.

I roll my eyes. If this keeps up, they might be screwing on this table by the end of the night. At least it can handle the body weight. I know from experience.

I should pass on another drink. I've probably already had one too many. Despite my best attempts at being good company to Michelle, I'm a mess of frazzled nerves. The foreign object inside an extremely intimate part of me is one thing. If it were just that, I'd likely be fine. I trust Gabriel with my body, and I know that whatever we're going to do later, I will enjoy it.

What I don't trust him with is my heart, and I'm beginning to worry that he has somehow managed to wrap his sinful fingers around it.

Something is shifting between us. It started last night, in that haze of intimate, sleepy sex, and while I can't define what it is yet, I know it's the last thing I expected or wanted—to look at him differently. And now we've just gone through this roller coaster of bloody shirts and is-he-or-isn't-he-a-murderer and him divulging crime family activity that you don't tell the woman you're just fucking, even if you've paid a shit ton of money for her.

And here we are, things shifting further. Becoming more intense. He wants my heart?

I'm not sure a man like Gabriel knows what that means. The way to a woman's heart is definitely *not* by bribing her to sleep with you.

But maybe he wasn't expecting this shift between us either.

What's even more bothersome is that he's told me about his involvement in the illegal prison fight ring and I don't care. That he divulged something like that to me is an odd source of pride.

How messed up am *I* to be proud of that? What is happening to me?

I let my gaze drift toward the wall of mirrors that reflects the strobe lights and cage dancers but reveals nothing more, and that gnawing feeling in my stomach stirs.

I'm *worried* about Gabriel.

I don't want to be worried about this man. He doesn't deserve my concern, and yet I can't help myself.

"So? Where *is* Gabriel and his sexy slut brother anyway?" Michelle hollers as soon as Dwayne is gone. She's on her fourth martini, and I'll likely be carrying her to her bed.

"In their office. They're meeting with someone right now. I don't know. It sounded important."

"We should go up there and interrupt their little 'meeting.'" Michelle air quotes that word with her fingers.

Memories of the tension in Caleb's face when he stormed in there has me shaking my head. "Yeah. That would be a bad idea."

"Oh right. Because they're basically the mob." Her eyes widen dramatically.

"*Michelle* ..." I glance around. It's too loud for anyone to hear anything, thank God.

A catchy dance song begins pumping over the speakers, and she throws her hands up with a squeal. "Let's go and dance!"

I sigh at my harebrained friend. The idea of going back out on that dance floor right now is *so* not appealing to me. The muscles deep inside clench as I begin shimmying across the bench, breathing steadily against the pressure. I'm not about to tell Michelle that Gabriel put a plug inside me, and I nearly came while on the dance floor earlier. I'm sure as hell not going to admit that the anticipation of being naked with him again has my panties soaked and that I'm eager to see Gabriel as much to know that he's safe as so I can get relief.

A horde of tall male bodies approaches from the left, stalling our retreat to the dance floor. Gabriel is leading the charge, followed by those two men I passed on my way here,

Caleb, and a few bouncers that made the group look all the more impressive. And lethal.

I only have eyes for Gabriel though, his collar unfastened another button, his face as handsome as ever, though stony. Whatever that meeting was about, I can't tell if it went well. It must have, if he's coming out here with the men now.

A rush of heat floods my core.

Michelle scoots over and leans in to press her mouth against my ear. "What. The. Hell. Merce! You didn't tell me how hot *all* his friends are!"

"Friends" probably isn't the right word for what they are, but I can't blame her for her reaction. The group is turning heads all around us.

"Which one is Caleb?" She waves the question off with her hand. "Actually, never mind. I'll do any of them. All of them."

"After Dwayne, of course."

"All in a good night's work," she says with mock seriousness, smoothing her palms over her black lace dress. "God, when did I become such a perv?"

Probably around the same time I did. Right around the time Gabriel stepped into my life.

He drops down into the booth, blocking my exit, shifting closer to me. "Hey, baby. Sorry that took so long."

I inhale the scent of his cologne and find myself sighing. "How'd it go?" I peer over to see the man with blue eyes and beard and the sleeve of tattoos eyeing me, his expression cold and calculating.

"Better than I expected. But, more importantly"—his gaze skims my dress, stalling on my chest. I wonder if my nipples are showing through this silky material. I don't dare check—"how are you?"

"Fine."

"Really? Just fine?" He presses a soft kiss against my lips, his tongue teasing over the seam, stealing my gasp. But he doesn't deepen it. Instead he turns to match the bearded guy's stare.

"Why do I feel like you're marking your territory right now?"

"Because I am." He leans in to press his mouth against my neck, just under my ear. "How wet are you?"

My heart begins to race as everything and everyone else disappears, all my attention on this sexy, all-consuming man beside me. I swallow, struggling to temper my voice. "I'm basically the Sahara."

His responding laugh sends a warm shiver down my spine. Beneath the table, he smooths a calloused hand over my bare leg, traveling up my thigh toward the hem of my dress.

I hold my breath, expecting him to dip his fingers into my panties and prove me a liar, but he settles his hand on my knee instead, and leans over to greet Michelle with a nod. "Welcome back. I take it Dwayne is taking good care of you?"

"If you mean blocking my opportunity to meet the man of my dreams, then yes, you should give him a big raise," Michelle quips, but then her eyes are flittering from Gabriel to Caleb and to the wall of eye candy behind.

Lulu the blond server comes around then with our two dirty martinis. When she sees Gabriel and Caleb, the fake smile she's been wearing all night for us turns genuine. She winks at Gabriel and then sidles up to Caleb and says something I can't hear, but it makes him grin and shrug nonchalantly.

Caleb nods toward the drinks. "Theirs?" I read off his lips.

"Yeah," she mouths, and while I can't hear her, I'm imagining that her voice carries a bitter twinge.

He steps back as if to allow her to do her job. Or to direct her to do it. Flashing him a lascivious look, she leans over the long oval table to set the drinks in front of us, far enough that I can easily peer down the cleavage of her impressive, store-bought breasts. I'm not sure she's even wearing a bra. What I *am* sure of is that the men behind are also getting an eyeful from the other angle. She makes a point of widening her stance.

Good grief.

I'll bet she makes a ton in tips.

There's no doubt in my mind that both Caleb and Gabriel have slept with Lulu. Countless times, probably. There's also no doubt in my mind that she may be a dick-swapper but she's also insanely jealous right now, hence the saltiness toward us all night. I mean, a VIP table, a personal guard, open tab all night ... she's figured out I'm not just another nightly fuck for him.

Whatever. She can still have Caleb's dick, but she can't have Gabriel's until I'm finished with it. Something she needs to learn and quickly.

I can't help myself. I lean in and press a soft, slow, tantalizing kiss against his lips.

When I pull away, he's smirking. "Why do I feel like you're marking your territory right now?" He echoes my earlier words.

"Because I am." I match his steady gaze. "Have you fucked her?"

"Yes," he admits without hesitation.

I expected the answer and yet it feels like a punch to my stomach. "Are you going to fuck her again?"

"Not while I'm with you."

But he will again, *after me*. After *us*.

Why does that thought leave me so unsettled?

His gaze locks on my mouth as I take a sip of my martini and try to push the distress away.

Caleb is saying something to Wayne, who then quickly moves in to lead the other men to the table across from us. Not that they couldn't all fit in here, I note. He directs Lulu to them with a slide of his hand over the small of her back and then settles into the booth on Michelle's other side. His eyes zero in on my best friend as he eases his way closer, his lascivious intentions plastered across his face.

"Hey, Michelle?" I lean in to say in her ear, "Remember when you asked me to stop you from kissing frogs? Well, you're about to screw a warty toad. Don't say I didn't warn you."

"Yeah. I don't care. I'll make him double up." She toys with the stem of her glass as she gazes dreamily at him.

"This is beautiful." Caleb reaches up to drag his fingertip over the delicate diamond and emerald necklace decorating her collarbone.

She shudders. "Isn't it? It's one of our new pieces. My family owns Banks Jewelry in Scottsdale."

I miss his response, distracted by Gabriel's hand sliding between my thighs, his fingertips rubbing over my damp panties. "Fuck." His chiseled jaw tenses. "When will you just admit you want me?"

I swallow hard. "Where's the fun in that?"

"Open for me."

"I told you, no shows," I retort, even as I fight the urge to obey and part my legs. The VIP section is designed in a way that offers privacy, with dark alcoves and deep tables and heavy curtains draping the sides. I can't see below the table across from me and I have to assume they can't see me.

The only person who might catch a glimpse is Michelle, and she's too enthralled with Caleb right now to care. Besides, nothing shocks her.

"Please, Mercy," he growls, though he's already working his fingers beneath the seam of my panties, prodding my thighs apart. I gasp as he pushes two fingers into me.

Shifting my legs farther apart, I let my eyes casually roam the faces around us as the music pounds, to see if anyone has picked up on what Gabriel's doing to me below the table's surface.

The bearded man across from us is watching intently.

Gabriel peppers my jawline with featherlight kisses that draw a soft moan from my lips. "You've never been this wet with me before," he murmurs, stroking my clit with the pad of his thumb. "How close are you to coming?"

"Close," I admit, reaching down to seize his hand. A few minutes with Gabriel is all it takes to get me there. But, while that guy across from us may not be able to see anything, he can damn well figure out what's going on. "Not in front of him."

Gabriel's gaze follows mine. A deep growl escapes his throat, but he relents, slipping his fingers out. In the next second, he's seizing my hips and hoisting me onto his lap, my back to his chest. The plug shifts, rubbing something deep inside.

I try desperately to ignore the sensation as I take a sip of my drink.

He leans in, pressing his lips against my ear. "Imagine how tight it's going to feel with that *and* my cock inside you later."

I can't even imagine my body accepting all that, but I find myself growing eager to find out if it can. For now though, I bite my tongue and focus on downing my drink while enjoying the steady thrum of Ariana Grande's "Dangerous Woman." A perfect song for the moment. That's what Gabriel does to me—there is something about him that makes me crazy, something that pushes me beyond my limits.

"Trying to get some relief?" There's a gruff, teasing lilt in Gabriel's voice.

Only then do I notice that my hips are rolling to the beat of the music.

"I just really like the song." I peer back over my shoulder at him. While Gabriel's feigning calm, his breathing is erratic, his chest is heaving, and his eyes are dilated.

And his dick is hard against my ass.

I may be desperate for an orgasm, but at least so is he. Which one of us will break first?

I grind my hips hard against his dick to the rhythm, earning both our groans, because yet again that plug shifts inside me. This might be my new favorite game to play with him.

"My office. Now," he growls.

I smile, and I imagine it's equal parts sweet and victorious, because Gabriel is breaking first and it took only seconds. "I'm sorry, but I can't leave my friend here alone."

"She's with Caleb."

I give him a high-browed look. "Exactly."

"Caleb!" he barks.

His brother leans over, and they share a long, hard gaze. Michelle catches my eyes and shrugs.

After a moment, Caleb rolls his eyes but then holds his hands up in surrender.

"Caleb will get her home, unmolested. She's fine." Gabriel shifts me off his lap and climbs out of the booth, adjusting himself with a hand against his groin, not bothering to hide the move. Only he can stand there with a noticeable erection and not look ridiculous. He holds a hand out toward me, and I see the unspoken warning in it.

Whenever, whatever.

Why am I fighting this?

I wiggle out, tugging my hem down to avoid flashing the table across from us.

I don't even look back at Michelle, my attention rapt on the powerful man ahead of me as he grasps my hand. With a single nod toward the other table, he leads me to the stairwell, brushing off several people trying to catch his attention.

"No one comes up," he demands of the guy standing at the bottom, urging me ahead of him. There's no bouncer waiting at the top anymore.

I instinctively reach back to hold my dress down, but he swats my hand away. I head up the stairs, acutely aware of how close Gabriel's face is to my ass.

The heavy steel door is barely shut when he's charging into me, herding me against it. "You like to tease, don't you?" he rasps, his hands going for the straps of my dress, pushing them off my shoulders. The silk dress falls to the floor effortlessly, and then he's reaching for the clasp of my strapless bra and unfastening it. My breasts spill out, feeling heavy and full and aching for his touch.

He yanks my panties down, letting them join the dress on the floor and then Gabriel's taking steps backward, toward the desk, his gaze eating up my form, naked save for my red stiletto shoes. "Come here."

I can't help noticing the strips of tape over the window, the kind of thing you need when glass is about to break. It wasn't like that before his meeting "What happened?" I ask warily.

"Nothing." He unfastens his belt and zipper and shoves his pants and boxer briefs down. His erection juts out beneath the hem of his dress shirt, making my mouth water. He takes it in his palm. "Get over here *now*, Mercy." He winces as if in pain.

I keep my stride even and slow as I make my way over to him, feeling the vicious smile forming on my lips. I'm enjoying his raw need for me.

With a hard swipe of his hand across the desk, he clears the surface, sending several crystal glasses flying to shatter against the polished floor.

I barely have time to jump before he's grabbing me by the hips. "Bend over," he commands in a hard tone. For the second time tonight, I find myself sprawled over his office desk.

I check the reflection in the window in time to see Gabriel grab both sides of his shirt and yank, sending buttons flying in all directions. He tosses the ruined garment to the floor, leaving him standing behind me with his pants pooled around his knees and the rest of his perfect, powerful body bare.

It's the hottest thing I've ever seen.

And when I arch my back to give him a better angle, a heady guttural sound escapes his lips.

I half expect him to plunge right into me, but instead he leans over, pressing his chest to my back, his hot skin a shock compared to the cold surface of the desk. He brushes my hair to one side and drags his tongue over the nape of my neck. "You enjoy teasing me, don't you?" he murmurs, rolling his hips, his hard length pressing against the base of the plug. As if to remind me that it's there—as if I could ever forget—he jerks his pelvis forward, shifting it.

A moan escapes me, unbidden. "Who's teasing who now?" I whisper, bucking against him.

"Maybe I shouldn't give it to you yet. I like seeing you like this." His hands are on me, worming their way between the desk to cup my breasts, massaging them with steady strokes that make me more needy.

I close my eyes, reveling in the intensity of being this vulnerable.

"Are you ready to cum harder than you ever have before?" he whispers, pinching my nipples in tandem before rubbing the pain away.

"Yes."

His face is buried in my hair. He inhales deeply, as if absorbing my scent, his fingers weaving through mine above my head. I feel his head prodding my folds, searching for that wet opening without the help of a guiding hand. He finds it quickly.

I gasp as he finally thrusts into me, the combination of the plug and his girth forcing me to take several calming breaths.

"That's it, baby. Take it all in. You're gonna love it," he coaxes.

I'm panting as he sinks deeper and deeper into me, my body stretching wide to accept him, the plug shifting, the pressure building. It's not quite pain but it's also not quite pleasure that I'm feeling right now. I don't know if I'll be able to handle him going at me rough.

He releases my hands and pulls himself up to stand over me. "I can't wait to take this tight ass," he murmurs.

Jesus, I can barely handle this small plug he put inside me, let alone *that*.

"You should see this view."

"You talk a lot," I pant, daring to buck against him again, the move stealing a gasp from my lungs.

He chuckles. The pressure eases as he slides out, but it comes back with vengeance when he slams back into me. My lips fall apart in a silent scream, that pleasure-pain combination stealing my voice.

"No one can hear you up here, baby. Let it all out." He pulls out and plunges into me again, this time hitting that bundle of nerves deep inside. Thank God I'm already sprawled out on the desk, because the move buckles my knees.

Another deep plunge, and this time the sounds ripped from my lungs are audible and wanton. A thin sheen of sweat coats my back. My legs trembles.

But with each pull and push of his cock into me, my body opens up a little more, welcomes him more easily, until I've fallen into a rhythm of bucking backward, riding his dick, the words "more" and "harder" falling from my lips in moaning demand, my sex drenched with need.

Gabriel slams into me with powerful, expert thrusts, his cries growing louder and more desperate, his grip on my hips tighter as he hits my sweet spot each time.

There's little warning to the impending explosion—a tingle skittering down my spine, swelling deep into my belly and through my thighs, the urge to spread my legs as wide as humanly possible and expose my sex to him—and before I can utter a word, my orgasm rips through me. I cry Gabriel's name, unable to think as my stomach muscles tense and all those sensitive, private muscles inside convulse.

Somewhere in the midst of my crazy high, I hear Gabriel's guttural moans, his thick length pulsing inside me as he spurts his hot seed. The notion of that makes my core throb with pleasure. I can't help the satisfied sigh that escapes my lips when we've both settled, my skin flushed, my limbs pliable, my body sated.

"Are you going to tell me that was *just* okay?"

"No." I close my eyes. I don't even have the energy to lie to him.

He slips out of me, and my muscles clench at the sudden vacancy. But the plug is still there. "Hold still a second. Okay, baby?" I feel him fumbling with the base. With a gentle tug, he slowly draws it out. A clang sounds as he drops it into the single remaining glass on the desk. "Beautiful," he murmurs, his palms pressing against my ass cheeks, spreading me wide. I jerk slightly at the sudden feel of his tongue darting over the sensitive skin there, but I'm too spent to squirm away. Gabriel's free to do whatever he wants to my body at this point.

But that seems to be all he wanted. He gives my ass a playful slap and then steps away to pull up his pants and fasten the zipper. With reluctance, I haul myself up. Now that the heady moment is over, standing in Gabriel's office stark naked feels awkward. What if Caleb were to barge in here? Gabriel didn't lock the door this time around.

I duck into the office bathroom to clean up and then head for my pile of clothes, gingerly slipping my panties back on. I cringe at the feel of the wet material. "I'm going to have to start carrying around extra panties as long as I'm with you," I mutter, fastening my bra.

"Or just don't wear them at all," Gabriel retorts with a

smug smile. He fishes his shirt off the floor, scowling at the missing buttons.

"That's two ruined shirts in twenty-four hours," I remark. This one, by his own hand.

He sighs and tosses it into the trash.

"Don't worry. This is a good look for you." I waggle a finger at his topless form. "I'm sure your patrons will appreciate it. You can bring a few fresh women home."

"You finished with me already? Can't handle a full month?" He laughs and opens a closet door where several more shirts hang. He pulls out another button-down and yanks it on.

My curious eyes wander to the tape on the window. "So, what happened up here earlier? During your meeting?"

"Just Caleb and his temper." He doesn't bother following my gaze. He knows what I'm talking about.

"Yeah, I wasn't expecting him to have one." I've only ever seen the easygoing playboy, unfazed by anything. I slip on my dress. The silky material doesn't have a single crease in it, despite the heap it was left in.

Gabriel snorts. "You have no idea."

I hesitate. "Who are those two guys?"

"Nobody you want to know." He fumbles with the buttons. "Caleb always buys these stupid shirts with the tiny little buttons. Who the hell can do these up?"

"Here. Let me." I wave him over. "I have much smaller, daintier hands."

He complies, wandering over to stand before me, his broad, hard chest bare.

I can't help but smooth my palms over the plane of muscle once before I begin working on the bottom buttons, thinking it's a shame to hide such a beautiful body. "So who's Camillo Perri?" Besides someone who apparently had something to do with his mother's death.

He curses under his breath and then shakes his head. "He's *nobody*. Forget you ever heard that name."

"Okay, fine, I just ..." I abandon the buttons to smooth my hands over his pecs again, my worry for this man flaring again. "You're not doing anything dangerous, are you?"

He blinks. "Why are you asking me that?" There's a distinctive shift in his tone to one of calculating calm. One that sparks a voice inside my mind, warning me to tread carefully here.

Don't ask, don't tell.

I shrug. "It's just Caleb said something the other day about you getting in over your head. And now there are these guys showing up and that cracked window, and that thing Caleb said about your mother—"

"Drop it, Mercy. I mean it," he growls, the edge in his tone as sharp as the shattered crystal tumblers on the floor. "Ignore anything he's said and anything you've heard. And don't ever repeat a word of it. Understood?" When I don't answer immediately, he barks, "Do you understand?"

The mood in the room has turned frigid.

Caleb isn't the only one showing me another side of himself tonight. And this version of Gabriel, I think I like less than the arrogant ass at Fulcort.

"Yup. Got it," I answer crisply, finishing off the last two buttons while avoiding his steely gaze, though I want nothing more than to tell him to dress himself. And go fuck himself. I can't ignore this burn of hurt I feel inside, which only makes me angrier.

"What do you care if I'm doing something dangerous, anyway?" he asks after another moment, his tone a touch softer. But only a touch. "You've already got your money for your father. That's all you want me for, isn't it?" I could be mistaken but the words seem tinged with bitterness.

His question gives me pause.

What if Gabriel were to tell me right now—right this minute—that I'm free to walk out that door, go back to my shitty apartment with Rob and Trisha trying to kill each other on one side and Dorito Glen masturbating on the other side, and continue struggling with this thing called life. That I've met my obligations to him and will never see him again. My dad will still be protected, and his legal fees are paid for, care of the money in that account.

That would be utopia, wouldn't it? That's what I would want?

The odd, unexpected tightness in my chest tells me that it might not be such a simple answer anymore.

And *that* tells me that I am seriously messed in the head. I don't even know this man.

But I think I'm beginning to want the opportunity to get to know him.

I swallow the flurry of conflicting emotions. "And all you want is my body, so I guess we're even."

He presses his lips together. For a moment, it seems like he's going to respond, maybe argue with me. But then he strolls away briskly, tucking his shirt into his pants as he walks across the office. He grabs his keys and wallet from a shelf by the door. "I've had enough of this place for one night. Time to go home."

I RETURN to my desk after a hellish morning to find an angry text from Michelle.

Michelle: Have you talked to that shithead yet?

I groan. Gabriel promised Caleb would get her home—safely and unmolested. But this is Caleb.

Mercy: No. Why? What did he do?

The three dots dance across my screen and I picture her lying in bed—it's 11:00 a.m.—furiously tapping away on her screen.

Michelle: NOTHING! I practically climbed onto his lap and he turned me down! I thought you said he'd fuck anything! I'm anything!

"Seriously?" I frown. That's impossible. That would mean Caleb has a decent bone in his body.

"How's it going with you today, girl?" Marsha comes around the corner into my cubicle, her brow pulled tight. "Did you get any sleep last night? You look exhausted."

I quickly mute my phone and tuck it away. "I was up late, studying," I lie, hoping the smell of alcohol isn't still seeping from my pores. It was almost two by the time we pulled into Gabriel's garage, the drive home tensely silent save for the sportscaster on the radio droning on with the day's highlights. Gabriel disappeared into his home office while I hopped into the shower. I drifted off wondering when he'd come to bed.

When my alarm went off this morning, I considered calling in sick, something I've only done once in all the years I've worked here. But that would mean dealing with Gabriel.

Given the morning I've had, I think dealing with him might have been easier.

I arrived to a pool of water in one of the counselors' offices and in not one, but two meeting rooms, thanks to the monsoon early this morning and our shitty roof. I've spent hours with Ali, our receptionist, mopping it up.

"Oh, right. When exactly are those exams again?" Marsha asks.

"Next week."

"And then you're done."

"And then I'm done," I say with an exhausted sigh. I hope. I still need to pass.

"Atta girl. I'm so proud of you. Life has thrown you a ton of lemons, and you are making some mean lemonade with it, aren't you?" She gives me one of her wide forced smiles, the kind that morphs into a wince. "So listen, I have another lemon to throw at you. The toilet's acting up."

I toss my pen haphazardly across my desk. "*Again*? He just fixed it!"

"No, that one's fine. It's the other one now." She gives me a look and then sighs. "See if you can get that plumber in this afternoon, will ya? Having two working toilets is critical with all the people coming in and out of here."

"Yeah, okay, but we haven't paid the last two bills from him. I don't know how willing he's going to be to do more work."

"Work that charm I know you have."

"I need that charm for a roofer," I mutter. In between mopping I was on the phone haggling with several, searching for one who'd be willing to patch a roof now and take payment in a few months, out of the goodness of his heart. I sink into my chair. "We're running bare bones, Marsha. I'm trying my best, but I don't know how to keep making this work."

Marsha sighs heavily and fumbles with the jade beads of her necklace. "Monsoon season is almost over. We can ride it out."

"No, it's not, and no, we can't. Sara lost all her files. Thank God she took her computer home or we'd be looking to replace that, too. Plus, the electrician is threatening to send our bill to the collection agency." I lower my voice, stealing a glance around to make sure no one's listening. "We can't settle all our debts and pay for everyone's salary next month."

Marsha purses her lips tightly. "Let's not worry about that right now, okay? Just get the plumber in to take a look and give us a quote. You do what you can and then you focus on your exams. It's all going to work out for you, no matter what. Okay?"

It doesn't take a genius to read between the lines. This building is falling apart and we're falling farther into debt. She created this office manager job especially for me six years ago and said she'd keep me on as long as she could afford to.

It's becoming obvious that she can't afford to anymore. She just can't bring herself to let me go—or even discuss it—until after I've finished my exams. Knowing Marsha, she'll take a hit to her own paycheck before she has "the big talk" with me.

I watch her amble away, her keys jangling in her pocket with each step, leaving me not only tired but in a sour mood now. I can't believe I'm so close to graduating with my degree and I'm about to lose my job at the place I feel most comfortable working.

With a sigh, I make the call to the plumber—he doesn't answer; I wouldn't be surprised if he's blocking this number—and then I head to the staff kitchen to heat up the enchiladas I found in the fridge this morning. Gabriel *did* say to help myself to whatever was in the fridge.

Back at my desk, I do what I've been waiting to have a chance to all morning, what's been dwelling in my thoughts since last night, that I can't just let go: I open up my internet browser and I do a search for Vlad Easton's wife and her car accident.

The first few articles that show up are about Gabriel's father and his criminal history—basically, what I've already read.

The fourth headline, dated September 2, 2000, is one that didn't appear in my original search.

It's one that turns my blood cold.

"Oh my God," I whisper, abandoning my lunch to scan the page, my hand over my mouth to muffle my gasps, my horror growing with each new line I devour.

Gabriel's mother didn't die in any car accident.

Not unless Gabriel's version of a car accident is being brutally raped and beaten before being shot execution style and left naked in a ditch for a motorist to find on his way to work.

Gabriel's mother was murdered.

No wonder Gabriel and Caleb get tense whenever there's any mention of their mother. At least my mother drifted off in a peaceful, self-induced slumber. If I had to choose, I'd take her overdose over this any day.

This happened in 2000. Gabriel said he was ten when she died. Caleb is only two years older than him, from what I remember of something Gabriel said. What's it like to be ten and twelve, the sons of a crime boss, and have your mother die like this?

The article says that the police suspected it was a revenge kill by a rival crime family, given who her husband was. There's a related link to another article about the suspect in her murder. I click on it and my stomach drops.

The police arrested Camillo Perri for her murder.

The article shows a picture of a distinguished-looking older man with dark, wavy hair being led into a courtroom, banked on either side by men in expensive suits. His lawyers, no doubt. He definitely isn't one of the men I saw at Empire last night.

Those lawyers earned their money, it would seem, because the case against Camillo was thrown out based on technical mistakes by the police and a violation of his rights.

Camillo Perri walked away free and clear for the brutal murder, though I'm guessing he did it.

And now Gabriel and Caleb were meeting with other Perris about "business" last night. About an alliance.

An alliance for what?

Why?

My stomach churns as I type Camillo Perri's name into the search engine next, to find that he's a well-known California vintner with vineyards in Santa Barbara, Sonoma, and Napa. He's sixty-seven years old according to this article and married to a beautiful, blond wife who modeled in her teens and twenties and survived a terrible car accident about fifteen years ago.

They have four sons together.

Of course. Those had to be Camillo Perri's sons there last night. They were definitely related.

I begin flipping through the Google images, searching for a Perri family portrait. I almost give up, but one finally appears.

I immediately recognize the two on the left. Merrick and Vince Perri. Those are definitely the two men who were at Empire last night.

Why would Gabriel and Caleb do business with the sons of the man who most likely raped and murdered their mother?

"What are you getting yourself involved in, Gabriel?" I whisper to no one but my computer screen. Caleb's warning to his brother about Camillo Perri knowing that he has a woman in his life springs to mind then. I'm beginning to connect the dots here, and the image emerging chills my blood.

What have *I* gotten myself involved in?

I GET STUCK at Mary's waiting for the roofer to show, assess the damage, and give me a quote. Ironically, the cost to patch the holes is almost exactly my salary for next month. If that isn't a sign that I should ease Marsha's guilt and hand in my resignation, I don't know what is.

It's seven by the time I turn into Gabriel's driveway, tired and overwhelmed by the day and praying there isn't a horde of people to deal with.

Thankfully, only the Porsche and Lambo are parked out front.

My relief is short-lived though, when I realize that my Toyota is gone.

I find Caleb rooting around in the fridge, already dressed for the night in black pants and a crisp white shirt. A silver tie hangs loose around his neck. I noticed he was wearing a tie last night too.

"Where's my car?"

"In the junkyard, where it belongs. The towing guys came around noon today. Have you seen Rosita's enchiladas? I was sure we had some left."

"No. You're kidding me, right? About my car?"

He peers around the door at me with his dark blue eyes, and he has the nerve to look perturbed. "I'd say you've upgraded. What's your problem?"

"That was *my car*!"

He closes the fridge with a sigh. "Dammit. Gabe must have finished them off, that cocksucker. He knew I wanted them. I'm telling you, there's nothing like that woman's cooking."

"Billy could have fixed it!"

"Who's Billy? Fuck, you're still stuck on that piece of shit? Forget about it. I guarantee it's already gone through the compactor." He grabs a banana from the fruit basket on the counter and peels it. "Just keep sucking my brother's cock like you do and you'll have whatever you want. And you two still owe me, by the way, for getting your little blond friend home last night and *not* screwing her. She was all over me, too."

"Thanks for your chivalry." I head toward Gabriel's wing, my irritation increased tenfold. "She's pissed at you, by the way."

"I can't win, can I?" he grumbles through a mouthful. "See you at Empire tonight?"

"No. I have to study."

"Right. You're still in school." There's a pause. "Wait, why are you still in school? Shouldn't you be done already?"

I grit my teeth as I round the corner, hollering, "I ate the enchiladas for lunch. You're right, they were phenomenal!" I barge into the bedroom just as Gabriel is pulling up his dress pants, his broad chest bare, the scent of soap lingering in the air.

The sight and smell of him gets my blood flowing, and yet all I can think about is last night's tension and what really happened to his mother.

And how he flat-out lied to me about what happened to her.

"Hey." I dump my bags on the dresser.

His hands pause on his zipper, a curious frown on his

beautiful face. "Rough day?" He looks downright sexy with the hard ridge of his cock showing beneath his boxer briefs and his unfastened pants sitting low.

The view stalls my tirade, but only for a moment.

I guess he's no longer angry with me for asking questions.

I sigh. "If you call dealing with floods and broken toilets all day, figuring out that you're about to lose your job, and then coming here to find out that some asswipe junkyarded your car rough, then yeah, it was a rough day." I wander over to the window to take in the pool. Maybe a few laps before studying will help simmer my anger. "Did you know Caleb was going to do that?"

"He may have mentioned it."

"And you didn't stop him?" My voice is full of accusation.

"Why would I? You're never driving that thing again."

"Uh ... yeah, actually I *was* going to." Gabriel and I won't be playing house forever.

His bare feet pad softly on the tile as he approaches me. "And fuck the job. Why do you want to work in a shithole like that, anyway?"

"Because I'm helping people who need it. Have you ever tried that?" I snap, his lack of sympathy grating on my nerves. I shouldn't be surprised. These people need help in the first place because of people like the Easton family.

"I'm helping *you*, aren't I?" he says in an overly calm voice.

I snort. "Yeah. At a pretty steep cost, I'd say."

"That you don't seem to mind paying, if your screams last night were any proof." He seizes my hips and pulls my body back into him, rubbing his erection on my ass.

"I'm not in the mood."

"Give me a minute to get you there." His teeth graze my earlobe. "I told you I like it when you're pissed off at me."

I know what he's trying to do, and it's not going to work. "You lied about your mother. About her car accident," I blurt out.

Gabriel stiffens behind me.

"I looked it up online today. She was murdered, Gabriel. Raped and murdered, and now you're meeting with the sons of the man who likely did it—"

Suddenly I'm spinning around and being backed into the wall by a stony-faced Gabriel.

"Sounds like you were doing more than just dealing with broken toilets today," he says with an icy voice.

I lift my chin in challenge. I will not be intimidated. "Did you really think I wasn't smart enough to figure it out?"

"I thought you'd be smart enough to listen to me when I told you to forget what you heard. Stay out of it, Mercy." That last warning is delivered through gritted teeth.

"You promised you wouldn't lie to me."

"And you promised not to ask," he fires back. "You're not getting involved in this. It isn't anything I can tell you about."

That's disconcerting, given he was okay with telling me about the prison fight club. How much worse is this?

I swallow. "Can you at least tell me if Camillo Perri really did it?"

His jaw clenches. "You read the articles, didn't you? He got off."

"My guess is he had really good lawyers."

His hard gaze and lack of response answer me.

"Look, I don't know what you and Caleb are getting yourselves involved in—"

"That's right, you don't, and it's staying that way." He grips my chin with a firm hand, just tight enough to feel forceful but not to hurt me. Penetrating eyes stare back at me. "You are just another pretty little fuck of mine, who sees nothing and knows nothing," he says, enunciating each word. "*Do you understand?*"

"And yet last night you were demanding my heart. What a surprise," I throw back, forcing a smile to hide the fact that his harsh words hit me in the chest harder than I expected they would.

He sighs and trails the pad of his thumb over my bottom lip. "You're not hearing me—"

I slap his hand away. "I heard you just fine. Go fuck yourself."

He dives in, seizing my mouth with his in a forceful kiss that I don't reciprocate. It takes him a second to accept that I won't, that this isn't going to work, and his lips stall.

I jerk my face away. "Why don't you go find another one of your pretty little fucks for the night? I'm sure one of them'll be in the mood."

His eyes roam my features, his jaw tense. "If that's what you want."

"You don't really care what I want, Gabriel. Let's not pretend." I'm tired of playing this game.

"Fine." He grabs his shirt from the bed and his wallet from the dresser, and he storms out the door, hollering, "Don't wait up."

"I never do," I holler back. Suddenly, I'm sick to my stomach.

That went sideways quickly.

I FUMBLE FOR MY PHONE. It's 3:18 a.m. Half an hour since I last checked.

Three hours since I gave up on my failed attempts to study, tucked my books away, and shut off the lights.

Two hours since I packed all my things into a bag, intent on leaving in the middle of the night.

One hour since I convinced myself to wait until Gabriel officially releases me so he has no excuse for taking away those funds or removing his protective hand over my father.

Gabriel's not home yet.

I care that he's not home yet.

I *hate* that I care.

I care that his lips are probably on another woman's mouth right now, that his hands are bringing another woman pleasure, that he's stripping her, teasing her, making her orgasm, whispering all kinds of dirty, sexy things that make her want him more, which he was saying to me only last night. I burn with jealousy over the very idea of it.

And I care that whatever luster he saw when he looked at me seems to have dulled the moment I started asking questions, starting trying to get to know him. Basically, when I started acting like I'm more than just the woman who's warming his bed.

Fucking hell, this wasn't supposed to happen. I was not supposed to care about that asshole.

A hot tear slips free from the corner of my eye.

TWELVE
GABRIEL

"It's Saturday! Shut that shit off," I snap as an alarm clock goes off. Normally I don't even hear Mercy's alarm, which means it's not going off quite as early as it normally does, but it's still too fucking early, especially for a weekend.

Especially since I didn't get home from Empire last night until four and then spent another hour in the cellar with Caleb, laying out our plan of attack over shots of vodka.

My head is pounding, and it hurts to open my eyes.

"I'm sorry," Mercy whispers, reaching over to turn it off. She sounds genuinely apologetic, which makes me want to beg for forgiveness.

With my tongue between her legs.

And after the way we left things last night—hell, the last two nights—I have a lot to apologize for. Does she know that I didn't mean what I said about her being nothing more than a pretty little fuck? That I was just angry and lashing out when I said I'd find someone else?

Has she figured out that I'm only trying to keep her safe?

"Hey ..." I reach for her, but she slips out before I can touch her. I paw at the vacant spot on the mattress, still warm from her body. It's only been a week and I can't imagine not having Mercy in my bed when I get home, even when she's pissed off at me. "Where are you going?"

"It's Saturday. I'm going to see my dad."

"You have all day to see him." Literally; visiting hours are from eight until four. "Come back to bed." My cock is hardening. What it'd give to feel her lips around it. That's the kind of early Saturday wake-up I can get on board with. Though, she may still be mad enough to bite down.

I'd deserve that.

"No, I don't. I have exams to study for. And I need to see him this morning. I'm not making him wait."

I listen to her feet pad toward the bathroom. A moment later the shower starts running.

Shit. She's actually doing this.

I was going to take her. There's no way I'm letting her go to Fulcort without me. I've seen firsthand the way the guards look at her. Especially Parker. That guy's a walking sexual harassment charge waiting to happen, except he'd probably get away with it, the way things operate over there. I'd like to think he's not stupid enough to try anything, knowing my interest in her, but the guy's got shit for brains.

It's not even 7:00 a.m. yet.

Fuck.

With a heavy groan, I haul myself out of bed and stumble to the bathroom, the throb behind my eye almost unbearable. The steam is already billowing, and Mercy's pajamas are in a heap. I can just make out her naked form under the stream of water, but it's enough to make me stall. The shapely curve of her back leading down to her hard, round ass is something every sculpture should be capturing.

I relief myself at the toilet, brush the fuzz from my mouth, and then climb into the oversized shower stall.

She glances over her shoulder at me, and that's when I see her tired, puffy eyes for the first time. I figured she was up late studying. Studying, and pissed off at me, if her position hugging the very far edge of the bed when I came home is any indication.

But those aren't just regular tired eyes.

Those are "I cried last night" tired eyes.

Her dark gaze darts down, lingering on my erection for a few beats before she turns away. "What are you doing up?" she asks coolly.

"You're not going to Fulcort alone." My shower has two overhead sprays, but I sidle up behind her to share her stream of water, molding myself to her. The hot water feels like balm for my hungover ass. "I'm coming with you."

"I don't need a sitter. I can manage on my own," she argues, her slight, sexy limbs tense against mine.

"This is nonnegotiable." She shudders the second I cup her supple breasts in my palms and begin kneading softly. The shape of her body is becoming familiar to me, an unexpectedly thrilling notion. "I'm sorry about last night."

Her jaw tenses but she says nothing.

I press a kiss against her delicate shoulder. "I wasn't with another woman."

"I don't care if you were."

Liar. "I wasn't with another woman last night. I swear."

She turns to peer up into my eyes as if to weigh the truth in them.

"I haven't been with anyone since I met you. I haven't wanted anyone else. I still don't want anyone else," I admit, putting myself in a highly vulnerable position, one I don't put myself in for any woman. But Mercy is quickly becoming not just any woman. In fact, I don't think she ever has been, not from the moment I laid eyes on her.

She swallows hard and then nods. She begins to relax against me.

"It's safer for you if you don't know anything about anything. Do you get that?"

"Like you said, I'm just another fuck," she mumbles, lathering body wash on her sponge.

"Yes. I said that." I graze her hardened nipples with the pads of my thumbs. "I didn't mean it, though. Not how you think I did. It's better that anyone watching thinks you mean nothing to me."

"Like the Perris?" She asks tentatively.

I sigh. "Yeah, like them. But I don't think you have anything to worry about with those two that were there."

"Merrick and Vince?" When she sees my eyebrows arched in question, she smiles sheepishly. "I found a family portrait on Google. I recognized them."

"Of course you did," I mutter, though I'm not pissed. "You're more thorough than half the federal agents I've had to deal with."

It's her turn to arch her eyebrows.

"Standard protocol for being my father's son and all."

"*Right.*" She hesitates, as if afraid to ask. "But do *you*? Have anything to worry about from the Perris, I mean."

"No." *Not from them.* I have plenty to worry about from my own damn family, though I'm not about to tell her that.

That seems to appease her.

I brush aside the wet strands of hair that cling to her forehead. "What's going on? Are you starting to worry about me, Mercy?"

"No," she throws back too quickly.

Another lie.

I smile. "If I didn't know better, I'd say you're starting to care."

"About your dick staying operational, sure." Her voice is husky. "You're no use to me otherwise."

I release a breast to slip my other hand between her legs, testing her readiness with one finger inside. She sighs with the touch. She may be upset with me, but she's also wet for me.

"Let's make sure it is." Hooking my hand under her thigh, I lift her leg up to give me access. Angling my hips, I enter my personal, sweet heaven with a guttural moan.

"I need to wake up like this every day," I murmur, beginning a steady, soft thrust into her. It feels new and yet it's quickly becoming familiar in the best way.

Yeah ... I'm beginning to see why someone might want to tie themselves down to one woman for life.

"It feels like it's been forever since I came here last." She smooths her oversized T-shirt and jeans over her body, her expressive brown eyes taking in the visitor lobby of Fulcort. They narrow at the front desk.

"Look, it's your favorite guard," I tease.

She grumbles something about a pervert under her breath, earning my laugh. A dull ache still stirs behind my left eye from my hangover, but coming twice inside Mercy this morning in the shower was exactly the medicine I needed.

"Don't worry, he won't bother you." I settle a hand on the small of her back, stroking it once before urging her on. "Not anymore."

She eyes me a moment, and her lips part. Whatever she

was going to say dies on her lips as she steps forward. "Mercy Wheeler, here to see Duncan Wheeler," she recites, sliding forward her driver's license.

"What? No 'hello'? No 'nice to see you, Parker'? Come on, Mercy, I thought we were old friends ..." His words drift as he notices me standing there.

Yeah, I thought so.

He quickly jots down her information, enters it into the computer with his two fat index fingers, and then slaps a key on the counter and jerks his head toward the security gate.

She frowns. 'I don't have to wait out here?"

"Do you wanna wait?" he throws back, his eyes darting to me.

"Nope. Thank you." She glances at me.

"I'm right behind you," I promise.

"Okay. But remember ..." She gives me a knowing look.

I sigh. "I know." Her father can't pick up on anything. I got the entire speech twice on the way over here this morning.

With a nod and a small, excited smile, she rushes through.

Parker scratches the stubble on his chin. "I heard Chops isn't up for visitors today."

"Not here to see him." I already knew that. Luckily, he ended up in better shape than I thought. The doctor I sent in to check on him said he's got a bruised kidney and should be kept out of the ring for at least four weeks. Six to be safe.

He's fighting again in two.

"Get my father."

"You got it," he mutters, in the same tone that could deliver a "fuck you." I ignore it, because frankly Parker isn't worth my energy.

With a curious glance at the bank of lockers where Mercy dumps her purse and things, he asks casually, "What is she to you, anyway?"

Or maybe he is.

I lean over the counter and lower my voice so as not to cause a scene. "She's none of your fucking business. That's who she is." The last thing I need is Parker chirping about the woman Gabriel Easton seems to be obsessed with, especially around here.

Parker's hands go up in a sign of surrender. "Just wondering."

"Don't wonder. Don't talk. Keep your big mouth shut. Understood? Don't become a problem for me." I can see by the way Parker swallows hard that he can at least put two and two together. There are a few people within these walls who can connect me to Mercy. This dumb fuck is one, and he's a terrible gossip. Donny, but he's one of the few I explicitly trust. And of course, Frankie, the guard who had his hands all over Mercy.

He'll never make that mistake again.

THIRTEEN
MERCY

It takes everything in me to keep myself planted at our table and not run to my father as he hobbles in to the visitor room. His face has returned to normal size at least, save for the bruising and cuts. But overall, he's far from well, the orange jumpsuit hanging off him. How much weight has he lost in the time he's been here?

"Easy, girl," he coos as I wrap my arms around his neck. We're only permitted a brief moment for a physical greeting, and yet I can't bring myself to let go. "Okay, okay ... the guard's about to yell at us," he warns in a hushed whisper.

I pry myself off him, stealing a glance at the nearby guard, the same one who barked at us the first time here and threatened to take away visitation privileges.

When our gazes touch, he gives a small nod and looks away.

Huh. That's ... interesting. Maybe he's in a better mood this time around. "They let you in quick today." My dad eases into his seat. "What time did you get here?"

"Early," I lie.

"I was wondering if you'd make it."

"Of course I did. I told you, I'll come every Saturday."

He sighs. "Yeah, I know. I was hoping you weren't serious about that though."

I ignore that. "How are you feeling? Does it still hurt?"

He shrugs and then winces, answering my question. "I think they slipped something into me while I was in the infirmary to help with the pain. I asked the nurses and they promised that they didn't, but I don't know." He chuckles. "I felt pretty good back there for a few days. Too good for a guy as banged up as I was."

They probably did. Gabriel said they were going to get him some better painkillers, and I told him that my dad wouldn't take them on account of my mother's drug addiction, the one that killed her. It would be just like Gabriel to then have them slip it into my father's food or IV.

I realize that I'm not mad about it.

But I avert my gaze to the tabletop to hide the truth from my father. "Well, if they did, it sounds like it wasn't the worst thing they could have done. How's everything else?"

"To be honest, I'm really not sure, Mercy." His brow is furrowed with worry as he studies me. "A lawyer came to see me yesterday. A fancy, expensive-looking one named Justin DeHavilland."

"Oh?" It comes out sounding like a surprise. The look my dad gives me tells me he's not buying it, so I quickly add, "I wasn't sure he'd come so soon." And that's the God's honest truth.

Dad bites his bottom lip. "He said you approached him about taking my case on."

"Yes." I clear the wobble from my throat. "I did. I asked him if his firm would consider taking it on pro bono, and after he reviewed your files, he agreed." I practiced that explanation in my head the entire drive here. "He came highly recommended."

Dad frowns. "By who?"

My mind goes blank a moment. I didn't anticipate him asking that. My dad is a simple man and usually just accepts things as they come. Why didn't I anticipate that? "Mr. Banks," I blurt out, because Michelle's father is the only rich man I can admit to knowing who might know fancy, expensive lawyers. "He said Justin was good. The best." And then, just to pile on lie after lie, I add, "I think he might have called Justin and talked to him about it. They're in the same social circle." You know, rich jewelers and lawyers to crime families.

I'm going to need to call Justin after this visit to get our stories straight.

From the corner of my eye, I catch a sleek figure strolling in, in jeans and a T-shirt. I can't help myself, my gaze darts to Gabriel as it always seems to whenever he's in the room. The bags beneath his eyes are dark today. It must have been close to five when he climbed into bed, the faint smell of liquor following him. I pretended to sleep, though in truth I barely slept all night, waiting for him like some forlorn wife whose husband is out until all hours, my mind wandering through all sorts of horrible scenarios.

I'm so relieved I didn't have to come here alone. Gabriel could have come to Fulcort much later, after getting enough sleep to function, seeing as visiting hour wait lines don't apply to him. And, since he was insisting on me not coming alone, he also could have been an asshole and put up a fight to keep me at his house until this afternoon, when he was ready to make the trip.

He did neither. He dragged his tired, naked ass out of

bed and climbed into the shower with me to get ready, his body heavy with sleep as he fucked me slowly.

"I guess this means your big plan to apply to law school so you can save your old man isn't necessary?" my dad says, snapping my attention back to him just as Gabriel passes behind us, offering a wink. He's on his way to his usual table in the corner.

"Yeah, that's right. Thank God." I let out a nervous laugh. "Dad, this is amazing news. You have one of the best lawyers in the state taking on your case. We have hope again."

He smiles, but it's guarded. "How's school?"

I shrug. "Exams are next week. If all goes well, that's it. I'm done forever."

"That's so good, Mercy. I knew you could do it. That's ... good. I wish I could be there." He swallows hard. "You know, to see you wear one of those funny hats when you graduate."

A ball swells in my throat. "You never know. Maybe this lawyer can get you out in time."

Dad chuckles. "I don't care how good he is, he's not going to be able to get me out of here *that* soon unless he plans on breaking me out."

The heavy door for the prisoners buzzes open, stealing my attention. Several men in jumpsuits filter in, pausing to get their instructions. I frown at the guard with the clipboard doling the table numbers out. He's not the one who was there when my dad came in, but I definitely recognize him as the guard who let me in to see my dad in the infirmary that day. The one who searched me for weapons. The one who had his hands all over my breasts, all while Gabriel watched with daggers in his eyes.

Someone beat the hell out of him. His left eye is black and his bottom lip has an angry purple gash across it.

Did that happen in here? Did an inmate attack him?

As he looks up to direct the prisoner in front of him, our gazes touch. His eyes flash wide and then they abruptly shift, darting over to the far corner where Gabriel sits before promptly dropping back to the clipboard, as if he doesn't want to get caught so much as looking my way. He gives instructions to the man waiting, keeping his eyes down the entire time.

My stomach drops with understanding.

It wasn't an inmate who did that.

I seek out Gabriel and find his steady gaze is on me.

Channeling my best "what the fuck" questioning look, I glare at him.

He merely shrugs. One of those sexy, lazy shrugs.

"You know, some weird things have been happening around here lately, too, that I need to talk to you about," my dad is saying, pulling me back once again.

"Oh? Like what?" I feign casualness. *Besides that guard being pummeled?*

"I don't know exactly." His gaze drifts around the room. "The guards seem to be a lot nicer to me. I don't know if it's because they feel bad for what happened to me under their watch—"

"That must be it."

He makes a sound, but it's not one of agreement. "And the kitchen guy gave me an extra helping of meat last night. I don't exactly know what kind of meat it was, but he mumbled something about me needing to heal."

"Which you do."

He snorts. "They don't give a shit if we kill each other in

here, Mercy. And guys I don't know have been passing by, nodding at me like they know me."

"So, you're making friends."

Dad shakes his head. "I ain't making any friends in here. Crazy Bob says I must have someone inside covering my ass."

Not inside.

He watches me steadily. "How'd you get into the infirmary the other day to see me? I know you said it wasn't important, but I'm beginning to think that it might be."

"It's *not* important. What *is* important is that you're safe." I hesitate, but then dare reach out to grasp his hand.

Dad steals a glance toward the guard. "See? He's watching and he's not saying a thing."

I let go. That probably wasn't the best move right now, as I try to convince my father that everything's fine.

"Mercy, please tell me you haven't gone and gotten mixed up with anyone you shouldn't be so much as talking to?"

"I'm fine. Everything's fine," I answer evasively. "How are things with Fleet's cousin, by the way? He hasn't bothered you since?"

My dad's assessing gaze is locked on my face for so long, I begin to squirm. He must not have heard me. Maybe his injury makes him space out. I repeat my question. "How are things with—"

"Fleet's cousin is dead."

FOURTEEN
GABRIEL

I WATCH Mercy's eyes widen as she recognizes Frankie at the door, his mangled face focused on his clipboard. My guys were waiting for him outside his house that same night when he returned from his beer league baseball game. I wanted him to know that I know where he lives, but I told them to make sure his kids were in bed already. There's no need for them to see that.

I'm not a monster.

Mercy's gaze flips over to me and it's brimming with questioning surprise. Not anger with me though, from what I can see, and I know what angry Mercy looks like because I see it every day.

All I can do is shrug.

As if I wasn't going to make sure Frankie—and every other guard in here—got the message: don't fucking even think about putting hands on Mercy's body again. From the way the guards are walking on eggshells around her, I'd say the message has been received as loud as I intended.

Mercy's dad pulls her attention back to him, and I take a moment to watch and admire her beauty.

Could she actually be falling for me? For all the swagger I throw at her, I know I'm not half the man she deserves. I would never call myself decent. I've never strived to be. For a lot of women, it doesn't matter. For some women, the ones who aren't entirely clueless and can connect dots, who I am is what attracts them. That dangerous element and all that, I guess.

I've had countless women tell me they're in love with me. Sometimes it's midfuck, so I'll excuse them for that. But there's been more than one instance where I've had to deal with tears and hurt feelings because a woman didn't get the memo that said, no, sex does not equal love and, yes, I'm fucking other women too.

Those were in my earlier days. I've learned to weed those women out and stick with the "dick swappers," as Mercy so lovingly calls them. The Rainas and Lulus of the world, who may feel some level of ownership over me but aren't stupid enough to try and assert it. I'm not oblivious though. I could take Lulu or Raina or any of those women to a jewelry store and they'd drag me straight for the engagement ring aisle.

Meanwhile, Mercy would laugh in my face.

Will that always be the case? Or will she eventually be able to accept me for who I am? A man trying to change.

Mercy's face pales suddenly. My instant reaction is to get up and run to her, to make sure she's okay, but I keep my ass firmly in my seat because I promised her I wouldn't tip her dad off about us, and that would definitely be a red flag.

I know what this is about. Her dad just told her what happened to that shithead who's been attacking him. No doubt that news spread like wildfire in here. God only knows the versions that are circulating. The only thing that's certain—no one's going to believe that was suicide.

The other thing that's certain? No one's going to talk.

I almost told her, that night we were in the pool and she left to study. She asked about him and I nearly told her, but I held myself back. I wasn't sure how she'd take it. It can't come as a complete shock to her, can it? She seems to have a good grasp of who we are, even if I haven't come right out and admitted to anything.

The horrified look on her face right now has worry seeping into my bones. Maybe I should have told her. She was going to find out anyway.

I hold my breath and wait for her to look my way again, praying that when she does, I don't see pure hatred in her eyes.

"Gabriel."

I missed my father's approach. "Hey, Dad." I force my attention to him. I'll have to worry about Mercy's reaction later.

He sinks into the chair across from me, smoothing his hand over the front of his jumpsuit.

"I heard you met with our friends on Thursday night."

Of course you did. The fucker has eyes everywhere.

"Do they agree that we have a mutual problem that needs addressing?"

"They do." *Just not mutually with you.* Merrick and Vince flew home yesterday after hitting it off with a few of the girls from Empire and taking them back to their hotel suite for the night. From what Raina said, they were decent men and treated them well. Then again, she'd say the same of us.

"Is the meeting arranged?"

"Yeah. Next week." We agreed that a neutral location would be best and seeing as Caleb and I were planning on heading out to see the Mage location anyway, Vegas it is.

"See? I knew this was the right move." A rare, satisfied smile pulls at his saggy jowls. "We'll have our problem solved soon enough."

I stifle my laugh. Does he actually believe that? The cartels are like cockroaches—you squash one, but meanwhile there are four more scurrying in behind you, taking up their positions. They're here to stay.

"What does my brother have to say about it?"

"Haven't told him yet." For all we know, Uncle Peter will scheme to take us all out in one fell swoop so he can claim ownership over all our territory.

Dad's eyebrows arch. "Why not?"

I hesitate, the folded photograph that Vince passed along practically burning a hole in my pocket. It's a mighty big domino piece and once I play it, things will be set in motion. There will be no turning back, and there's also no telling how Dad will react.

Aside from violently.

"Because we don't trust him."

Dad scoffs. "He's family."

"Yeah. Like that cousin of yours." I pull the photo out and push it across the table wordlessly. If we were anyone else, the guards would be on us like flies on a pile of fresh dog shit. But we're us, and Donny's attention is conveniently elsewhere.

Dad sighs, muttering, "What is that?" as he reaches for it.

"Something we came across recently that you need to see."

His gaze drifts around as he unfolds it. He glares at it, his cold blue eyes narrowing. "What the fuck is this?"

"That was taken a day before—"

"I can see that!" he snaps. "Who gave you this?"

"That's our cousin in the front with the FBI agent," I say instead of answering his question. "And Peter's in the back."

Dad glares at the page for so long I half expect it to burst into flames. He knows what it means. "Where did you get this?"

"From Vince Perri."

"This is bullshit. They're trying to cause strife in our family again," he hisses.

"It's not bullshit, and you know it. Think about it." I keep my voice calm. Caleb and I expected this reaction. It was the same one we had. "You always wondered if there was someone else working against us. Someone betraying us." I tap the page. "There's your answer. He wanted you out of the way so he could take over everything."

Dad's fist closes around the page, crumpling it into a tight ball, his teeth grinding.

I give him a minute to absorb this before asking, "What do you want us to do?"

"Make sure that meeting is successful."

"What about—"

"Do as I say!" he barks, slamming his fist against the table. I sense the heads turning but I keep my eyes on him. He stands and strolls away, his back stiff with tension.

And now we wait.

FIFTEEN
MERCY

THAT ODD NUMB feeling still courses through my limbs as I hand the locker key to the security guard at the exit gate after collecting my things.

His gray, knowing eyes flash to me before dropping again. "Thank you, ma'am. See you next weekend."

How does he know I'll be here next weekend? Does he know who I am? Does he know what happened to Fleet's cousin?

I mean, of course he knows what happened. Everyone living within these walls does, according to my dad. Diego killed himself in solitary the night after I came here last, the night before Gabriel snuck me in to see my father in the infirmary. They're saying he used a belt to hang himself.

But where the hell did he get a belt from?

While *in solitary*?

There's another answer for it all, one that makes my stomach roil.

I sat in that little, white room and I asked Gabriel what he was going to do about my dad's attacker. I wanted to know what this "protection" meant. He asked me if I wanted details, if I cared. I told him that I didn't. I remember thinking I wanted the man dead for what he did to my father. I didn't voice it, but did I need to? Deep down inside, didn't I know what Gabriel's form of "protection" might mean?

In a way, I'm the one who ordered that man's death.

A thought that has left me feeling numb.

Gabriel is leaning against the concrete wall at the end of the hall ahead of me, his ankles crossed, his eyes closed as if trying to catch a few minutes' rest.

Waiting for me, clearly.

All I can think is, this man is dangerous.

I've suspected he was dangerous from the moment I met his stormy, dark eyes. His father, his money, everything about him screamed danger ...

I've always suspected, but now I have solid proof of it.

And yet I'm not feeling fear toward him.

What *am* I feeling for Gabriel right now?

He had that guard beat up for laying his hands on me, that much is clear. But it's nothing the man can't walk away from.

Fleet's cousin isn't walking away. He also can't hurt my father anymore. No matter how horrified I might be that the man is dead, my thoughts keep going back to that and it brings me overwhelming relief.

What kind of person does that make me?

Maybe I'm still in shock.

I steady my breathing as I approach Gabriel, unsure of what to say. Who knows what mood he'll be in. He left the visitation room twenty minutes before I did, after only a few minutes with his father. Whatever happened between them, it didn't look good. I caught the folded piece of paper that Gabriel slid across the desk. Gabriel's lips were moving fast, and the tension building in his father's shoulders with each second that passed was visible.

And then suddenly Vlad Easton was balling up the paper and banging his fist on the table, demanding that Gabriel do something. He stood and marched away without a backward glance at his son, his face as a mask of fury.

At who, though, I wonder. At his son?

Gabriel watched him leave with an odd calm about him before slowly standing and making his way out, passing by me with nothing more than a glance, an unreadable look painted across his face. He seemed unbothered.

I settle on, "Hey," when I reach him.

His eyes peel open, and I see how the whites are tinged with pink. He's exhausted. "How was your dad?"

"He seemed better. He had a lot of questions though."

"What'd you tell him?"

I shake my head. "Nothing true." It's for the best.

Gabriel stares at me a long moment as if trying to read my mind and weigh my thoughts.

His chest heaves with a slow, heavy sigh. "Ready to go?" He doesn't wait for my answer, lifting off the wall and sauntering down the hall toward the exit. We don't say a word to each other until we've passed through security and are almost at his car.

"Can you drive?" he asks.

"What?" I stare wide-eyed at the Lamborghini. "Are you crazy?"

"I can barely keep my eyes open. If I get behind that wheel, we won't make it home. So unless you want to hang out in the Fulcort parking lot while I catch two hours ..." He dangles his keys in the air in front of me.

I need to get home and crack the books. With a heavy sigh, I take the keys and head for the driver side, pausing to peel off the prison visitor garb I pulled over my tank top and shorts earlier.

"I really love it when you strip in the prison parking lot," he mutters dryly, shooting a glare at the guards watching. They promptly turn away, though not before flashing knowing smirks.

"Shut up. It's hot." I ball the clothes up and toss them in the back and then climb in.

"You can adjust the mirrors with that button on your left," he says, already reclining the passenger seat, getting comfortable.

I toy with the buttons to get the angles right for me. Meanwhile, I'm ready to burst with questions. "My dad told me Diego hanged himself in solitary."

He doesn't say anything for a moment. "He must have felt overwhelming guilt for his crimes." He says it so casually, his eyes closed.

"Gabriel—"

"Mercy." There's a warning edge in his tone. "Not now. Not here."

"Fine." I need to wrap my head around it anyway. I start the engine, and my stomach does a flip as the powerful engine rumbles. "Your visit with your father was short."

"He's not much of a talker."

I chew my lip, wondering if I should push it. "He seemed angry when he left." Yeah, I'm going to push it.

"He usually is. You know your way home?"

"Yeah."

"Good." His chair shifts another notch back, and he splays his legs. "Wake me up when we get there."

"Is everything okay?"

"Will be when you let me get some sleep."

I sense I'm not going to get any more out of him.

The car lurches forward, and I slam on the brakes on impulse. Shit. "I'm going to wreck your car," I warn.

"Don't." His lip twitches, his eyes still closed. "Unless you want to spend the next ten years sucking my dick to work it off."

I shake my head at his attempt at humor and ease the car forward gingerly this time, muttering, "My rates are high. Try six months."

His soft chuckle carries through the car.

Gabriel stirs from a dead sleep as I'm waiting for the garage door to open.

"You didn't trade paint with anyone." His voice is groggy.

"No, most people gave me a wide berth," I admit, smoothing my hands over the steering wheel. I'm not going to lie, I felt powerful on the freeway. All I had to do was think of going faster, and all of a sudden I was nearly doubling the speed limit. I had to force myself to slow down more than once.

Gabriel twists in his seat to peer out the back window at the line of cars. He sighs, the only sign that he might care that his brother is entertaining people in their house. The move brings his sexy, powerful body closer to me though, and that makes my blood race.

Christ. The man had a guy murdered and another one beaten up. I *should* be terrified of him, and yet I can't muster that fear.

What I am is still insanely attracted to him.

Maybe because I realize he did it all to protect me.

Maybe because he has given me some semblance of control over my life again. I've spent these last months—years, really—feeling helpless, with my father's predicament. Now, I'm getting help for him and *no one* is going to mess with me or my father in Fulcort. I feel anything but helpless and it's because of Gabriel.

I creep the luxury sports car into the garage and shut off the engine. The silence is deafening.

"You liked driving this, don't you?"

"Yeah," I admit. "It's powerful." Like Gabriel is powerful. I'm beginning to appreciate that part of him, despite the other parts, the ones I'm trying not to think about.

His dark blue eyes linger on my profile. "Are you okay?"

The million-dollar question. "Did you—"

"Not here." He cuts me off, but his tone is gentle. "We'll talk about it later. But just know that it's all to protect you." He collects my hand in his and brings my palm to his lips to press an unhurried kiss against it. "I will never let anyone or anything hurt you. Do you believe me?"

"Yes. I do." Maybe that's why I'm not terrified of him.

"Good. Come on. Let's get inside."

At least thirty people mill around the living room and main patio, laughing and talking while music pumps through the house speakers. I recognize some of the faces from the club on Thursday night.

Is this what all their life is always like? Just one big party, floating between here and Empire all weekend long?

"Gabe," Caleb calls out, strolling toward us with that leisurely swagger, a burger in his hand, his swim trunks hanging low on his hips. At least he's wearing shorts. "All good?"

Gabriel gives a single nod. I guess his dad's reaction was expected?

Caleb grins at me. "How's your Daddy-O?"

"He's good. Says you owe us a new car."

"Nah." He shakes his head and laughs. "He doesn't even know about me."

"Baby, we should put more burgers on," a soft voice croons. I turn to see a topless Lulu—the bitter blond server from Thursday night—wander over. She presses her breasts against Caleb's bare arm.

His blue eyes dip down to her erect nipples. "You think so?"

"Uh-huh." She turns to Gabriel, and her eyes twinkle deviously. "What do you think? Are you hungry?"

There's no way she hasn't figured out that Gabriel and I are together.

There's also no way she's talking about Gabriel eating a burger right now.

Fucking shameless.

I weave my fingers through his, partly to quell the urge to punch her in her perfect nose. "He's starving, actually," I answer coolly. "I'll make sure to feed him well."

Someone lets out a sharp whistle of appreciation as I lead a smug-looking Gabriel toward his wing.

"I thought you had to study?" he remarks with humor in his voice as we turn down his hall.

"I *do* have to study. I guess you'll just have to make it—" My words cut off as we step into the room to find the skinny redhead lying naked in Gabriel's bed, entwined with an equally skinny and naked blond.

"Oh my God!" I exclaim, stunned for a moment. It's eleven in the goddamn morning! I spear Gabriel with a glare. "Is this normal? You know what?" I hold up a hand.

"Never mind. Of course it's normal for you to find two naked women waiting for you in your bed!"

He shrugs. "I forgot to lock my door."

"And there aren't six other bedrooms to choose from?"

The two women don't have the sense to read the room, pausing to watch us with curiosity and not a shred of shame.

"Get out!" I growl, gathering the damp bathing suits strewn across the floor and tossing them out into the hall.

They both look to Gabriel, as if waiting for his instruction.

"Get *the fuck* out before I lose my shit!" My blood is surging through my veins as I rage.

They move quickly now, climbing off the bed and scurrying out the door.

"I'm sorry—" he begins, but I'm not in the mood for an apology.

"Whatever."

"I didn't tell them to—"

"You didn't need to. I'm sure you've come home to them in your bed a thousand times before, and you've always been more than happy to join them." Bitterness seeps into my tone.

He presses his lips together, not denying it.

"Yeah, I thought so." I turn, intent on hiding in the bathroom.

"Seriously, after everything that happened at Fulcort today, *this* is what you're pissed with me about?" He has the nerve to look pleased, which only fuels my anger.

"Yes!" I throw my hands up in the air. "Because this is going to happen *every* goddamn weekend! And what happens when I'm *not* here? Will your perpetually hard dick be able to resist?"

He smiles wide. He actually finds this amusing.

"Fuck you," I snarl. "Go away. I need to study for the next five days straight. *After* I burn the sheets." I don't mean to slam the bathroom door.

Okay, maybe I do.

Lord, what have I hitched myself to?

SIXTEEN
GABRIEL

FUCK, that woman is so goddamn sexy when she's mad. Just thinking about her now makes me want to blow my load.

She kicked me out of my room two hours ago. I could have been an asshole and insisted on staying, but I figured I'd let her calm down.

Plus, these burgers smelled too amazing to resist, and I'm starving.

I'm halfway to my room, a plate of food and a drink in hand, when Raina calls out my name to stop me.

"Hey." She trots up the steps, her skimpy, black bikini doing nothing to keep her tits from bouncing. "I'm sorry about earlier. We didn't know that you were ..." Her voice drifts, her doe eyes flashing toward my closed door.

"No worries." I offer her a warm smile. It's not her fault. Mercy was right—it's been standard practice around here for a long time, and they've never been kicked out before. "Just maybe move your party to Caleb's room from now on." The more the merrier, as far as he's concerned.

"Right." She bites her bottom lip, hesitating. "So, who's your girlfriend?"

"Her name is Mercy." I don't correct the girlfriend part.

"Is it, like, serious?" I can hear it in her voice. She's hoping I'll say no.

Raina seems so young and immature and lacking in this moment. All the women I've been with these past years have been young and immature and lacking. I could never pinpoint it though. I didn't know any different.

I didn't *want* to know the different.

"Yeah, you could call it that." The woman has invaded my every thought; she owns my dick; I've agreed to things and told her things that Caleb would pummel me to the ground for.

But the best part of all? I think she's beginning to feel the same way about me. Why else would she fly off the handle like that earlier?

Damn, she's got a temper.

"Well, you know I don't mind sharing you," Raina purrs, her small hand dragging over my stomach and down. She palms my cock through my swim trunks.

"Not gonna happen, Raina," I warn, continuing on my way to my bedroom.

I find Mercy stretched out on my bed, scowling at her textbook. Her sharp eyes size me up before darting to the plate in my hand.

"Figured you were starving." I set it on the nightstand.

"Thank you," she says curtly. Still mad at me.

Maybe I shouldn't have grinned at her the way I did.

I know I should let her get back to studying, but I'm reluctant to leave. My gaze wanders over the array of books and notes covering half my bed, looking for something to strike up a conversation. One that doesn't involve people in prison or me doing fun, dirty things to her body.

I notice a fresh printout. A letter to a Marsha Thompson, with Mercy's signature scrawled on the bottom.

I frown as I pick it up and scan it. "You're resigning?"

She doesn't speak for a minute, but then sighs and sets her textbook down. "Yeah." She reaches for her plate.

"Why?" Not that I care. This is actually good for me. It means I'll get to start my mornings right—between her legs at a reasonable hour.

"Because she carved out that job just for me, but she doesn't have the budget for it, not when the building is falling apart. It needs massive repairs."

"It *is* a shithole," I agree, earning her glare. I set the page down. "But why don't you just wait until she fires you. You'll get unemployment that way." My guess is that's important to her.

"Marsha won't do the right thing and let me go. She feels bad because of my father and school. She's letting it cloud her judgment. But she can't afford to pay me. It's as simple as that." She's shakes her head, tension radiating off her. "There are other addiction centers in Phoenix. It's just ... Mary's is the one that was there for me after my mom died. The people there have always been there for me. It's the best one. It's the one I want to work at." She sighs heavily. "Whatever. I can't think about that right now. I have to pass these exams."

As much as I'd like to shove these books off the bed, pull her shorts down, and give her a release she could use, I know that it won't help relieve her ongoing stress. The best thing I can do for her, besides hunting down those profs and making sure they pass her, of course, is to give her space.

"Study hard," I whisper, leaning down to press my lips against her forehead.

I feel her gaze on my back the entire way.

Look at me, being all unselfish.

Caleb's right.

I'm falling for this woman, and I'm falling hard.

SEVENTEEN
MERCY

It's almost 10:00 a.m. Marsha should be out of her meeting soon.

I hold my resignation letter in my grasp, rereading it for the hundredth time since Gabriel's home office printer spat it out. Quitting my job is the last thing I should be focusing on this week, but I know it's the right thing to do. Marsha will be relieved.

Once she stops refusing to accept it, that is. I'm hoping she suggests that she put it in as a termination, so I can at least collect enough money from unemployment to pay my bills until I can find something new.

I hear Marsha before I see her, the jangling costume jewelry and her heavy, rushed footsteps impossible to mistake for anyone else.

"Oh, hey, Marsha, I was just going to come and see—"

"You would not believe what the courier just handed me!" She exclaims, waiving a slip of paper in her meaty hand, oblivious to my sour mood.

I set my letter facedown and force a smile. I don't want to burst her bubble just yet. "What is it?"

"Mary's just got a donation for *a hundred thousand* dollars!" Her brown eyes light up. "That's more than enough to fix this old place up!"

"What?" I croak, playing that number over in my head. "Who's it from?"

"I don't know." She shakes her head, frowning at the check. "Some law firm ... DeHavilland, Arnold, and Gold issued it, but there was a note stating that the donor wished to remain anonymous. Who knows, who cares! We are back in business!"

Comprehension hits my stomach.

"Oh gosh, Mercy, you have no idea how stressed I've been these past few months. I wasn't sure how I was going to ... Well, anyway, we're going to be just fine. I may even be able to earmark enough salary for an additional part-time counselor. I heard there's a young lady who's finishing up her education soon." She winks at me, her excitement palpable. "Now, what were you saying when I barged in here? You had to tell me something?" Her eyes flit to my desk, drifting over the resignation letter.

"Plumber's coming at three today," I say, casually shifting a file folder to cover it.

"Oh, thank heavens. I'm going to run to the bank to deposit this now so we can actually pay him!" With a giddy wave, she charges off.

I let out a giant sigh of relief, even while so many conflicting emotions swirl inside. How am I supposed to take this? There's no doubt this is Gabriel's doing. I didn't ask him to do it. I didn't suggest or hint at it.

Honestly, I didn't even think to ask.

But he did it anyway, though he has trash-talked this place on plenty of occasions.

Appreciation swells in my chest, despite the sick irony

of how that money likely arrived in his bank account in the first place.

Mercy: Thank you. You're doing a lot of good for a lot of people.

I'm busy tearing my resignation letter up into tiny pieces when my phone chirps with a response.

Gabriel: What can I say, I'm a philanthropist.

I snort.

Gabriel: I need you to take Thursday and Friday off.

Mercy: Why?

Gabriel: Because I'm taking you somewhere.

Flutters stir in my stomach. I bite my lip as I consider his request. I write one exam tonight and the other on Wednesday. God knows I could use the break. And aside from the days I took when my father was on trial, I've never asked for any vacation days off.

Mercy: Where?

Gabriel: It's a surprise.

Mercy: Only if you let me study, uninterrupted, before then.

Gabriel: Haven't I been good so far?

He really has. Aside from bringing me meals and drinks, I've barely seen Gabriel since Saturday. I actually miss him.

Gabriel: Say yes.

I grin as I tap out my answer.

Mercy: Yes.

I hesitate before I send the next message.

Mercy: Make sure you're there when I get home tonight.

Gabriel: Why?

Mercy: It's a surprise.

So MANY YEARS, so many exams.

And as I step out these heavy, glass doors for the last time, I feel weightless.

"How'd it go?" Ben asks, sidling up beside me.

"Well. I think it went well." I sigh with relief. "Thank you for studying with me. It made all the difference." We spent all Sunday at the library, quizzing each other and going over past exam questions until my brain was swimming.

He slides his hands into his pockets. "So I guess this is it."

"For school? *Yes.*" I let out a breathy laugh. And to think, I nearly signed up for another four years of it in law school. "But I'll call you."

"Sounds good." His head bobs eagerly, and then his eyes drift to a spot behind me. "I take it that's for you?"

I turn around in time to see an SUV with tinted windows pull up next to the curb.

Gabriel steps out of the back seat in his typical sexy Empire attire—though it's Wednesday—and gives me a subtle nod.

I've been so consumed with studying that aside from an hour-long shower with him on Monday night, complete with a happy ending for both of us, I've barely talked to him. He's made himself scarce.

Now, the sight of him makes me giddy. "It is. See you around, Ben." I practically float down the steps.

Gabriel is smirking when I reach him. "I take it the exam went well? Or are you just that excited to see me?"

I fight the urge to sink into his chest, but I can't help my grin. "Exam went well. But I'm starving now."

"Good. They have great food where we're going."

"And where is that?"

He gestures toward the back seat. "You'll see."

"Could you be more evasive?" I ask, attempting—and failing—to sound annoyed.

"I could," he teases, and that dimple appears. "Come on."

"But what about the Lincoln? I can't just leave it here."

"Already taken care of. Get in. We have a flight schedule."

A *flight* schedule? I climb in, noting the two small suitcases tucked into the far back. "So, we're going *away* away?"

He slides in beside me and pulls the door shut. He nods at the driver, and the SUV pulls away. "We're going to Vegas. Rosita washed and packed all your things for you."

"Vegas?" I can't help the excited twang of my voice. I've always wanted to go.

"Yeah. Caleb and I are checking some property we're thinking of buying and I thought you might like to get away."

"This ... yeah." The prospect of doing something so spontaneous is overwhelming. A thought strikes me. "But when will we be back? Because my father is expecting me on Saturday."

"Don't worry, we'll be back on Saturday. It's a short flight." He slides his hand into mine, his calloused palm deliciously rough against my skin.

I can't help but stare at where our hands are joined. Of all the heady, sexy things we've done, Gabriel simply holding my hand feels the most intimate.

"What's that look for?" he asks, his brow furrowed with amusement.

"Nothing. This all just feels very ...," *Boyfriendish* ... *Lovey-dovey* ... I settle on, "date-y."

He smirks. "What are you saying? That we can't go on a date?"

"Would you even know how?"

"There's *nothing* I can't do with a woman." He eyes me curiously. "Mercy, I've had my tongue in your ass. Why couldn't we go on a date?"

I nearly swallow *my* tongue as my eyes flash to the driver, my cheeks burning bright.

Gabriel chuckles softly. It earns him a sharp elbow to his ribs.

"For starters, because you say things like *that*," I hiss. "I doubt you could restrain yourself and do something *normal* like just hold a woman's hand for a night."

"Of course I could," he argues.

Yeah, I'll believe it when I see it," I mutter and let out a derisive snort.

His eyebrow arches. "That sounds like a challenge."

Caleb is on his phone and pacing around another black Escalade when we pull into the airfield. A small private jet sits on the tarmac ahead of us, the door propped open. A nervous flutter stirs in my stomach. I wonder if this is the right time to tell Gabriel I've never been in a plane.

"What took you guys so long?" Caleb hollers when we step out.

"Construction, sir," our driver explains, heading for the back to collect our luggage.

"Relax, we're only fifteen minutes behind." Gabriel's fingertip trails down my spine. "You good, Mercy?"

"I'm fine," I answer, my tone clipped. I'm so goddamn horny, I can barely stand my own dirty thoughts.

Gabriel likes to prove points. This is something I'm quickly learning. Today's point was that he is fully capable of simply holding my hand and nothing more. It was unexpectedly sweet at first, as he weaved his fingers between mine and settled our joined hands on his muscular thigh on our way here.

I rolled my eyes at him but humored him by allowing it, offering a small smile.

But then the rhythmic stroking began. Slow, smooth strokes of his thumb to the beat of the music playing over the speaker, over my palm and my wrist. Soft drags of the edge of his fingernail, biting into my skin with just the right amount of pressure that it couldn't fade into the background, couldn't go unnoticed.

It wasn't long before I found myself closing my eyes and imagining that skilled thumb stroking my bottom lip, the hard buds of my nipples, my swollen clit ... and Gabriel proved even something as simple and innocuous as holding his hand could become a dangerous thing.

"Surprise!" a familiar voice shrieks.

My libido is temporarily doused when Michelle jumps out of the back seat of the other SUV. "Oh my God! What are you doing here?" I exclaim, my mouth hanging open.

She throws her arms around my neck. "Celebrating you *finally* being done with school! I'm coming to Vegas with you! I brought so many dresses!"

Warmth fills my chest as I return the hug. "Oh my God, this is so amazing."

"Caleb came by my place Monday night to ask me."

"Really?" I shoot him a glare.

He holds his hands up in surrender, but he's grinning like the Cheshire cat.

"I asked Caleb to reach out to her," Gabriel explains. "I figured you might want a friend there."

"Hey!" One of the twins—Felix, I think—pops his head out of the open door of the jet. "You guys ready to go or what? We're waiting!"

"Hot damn." Michelle's eyes widen at the sight of him. "Who is *that*?"

"Nobody while I'm around, sweetheart." Caleb ropes his arm around my friend's slim shoulders, pulling her into his muscular chest, his smirk downright devilish.

Gabriel leans in to whisper, "Do you want to tell her that she can have both of them, or should I?"

"Shut up," I scold, but I'm laughing. What happens in Vegas and all that ...

Gabriel presses a soft, lingering kiss against my lips.

This is not how I anticipated celebrating the end of school. I must admit, it's a million times better. "Thank you for doing this. It was very thoughtful." Something I'm learning Gabriel is abundantly capable of, when he wants to be.

He pulls me flush against him, and my body aches for the hard length pressing against my stomach. "Is it *normal* enough for you?" He mocks.

"*Nothing* with you is normal, Gabriel." From his incarcerated mobster father to the means by which his family "allegedly" makes their fortune, to the depraved bribery scheme that got me here in the first place... it's about as far from normal as anyone can get.

Then again, my life up until now wouldn't exactly be labelled "normal" either.

"I'm trying, Mercy. I really am." Gabriel bends to touch

his forehead against mine. "We're going to look at a hotel and casino to buy."

I laugh. "That's *so* the opposite of trying to be normal." He really has no clue.

A cute, sheepish grin touches his lips. "Yeah. I know. It's big. But if we can pull it off ..." His jaw tenses, his hesitation to continue that sentence obvious. "It'll be just Caleb and me, one-hundred-percent legit. We won't be involved with *anything* else." He gives me a knowing look. "We both want away from it. We've wanted away from it for a long time, but when you have family ties like we do, it's not easy."

It's the most he's ever divulged, the closest he's ever admitted to being tied to the drug trade. "Why are you telling me this?"

"Isn't it obvious, Mercy?" His deep blue eyes are oddly bright. "Because you were the final push for me. I want to be better *for you.* I want to deserve you."

I swallow the rising lump in my throat. For all of Gabriel's dirty talk and arrogance, hearing him speak so frankly, so earnestly, threatens to weaken my knees.

But what would Gabriel need to do to "deserve" me? What would I accept? I can't begin to wrap my head around the answer to that. He wants to build himself a new life, a "legit" life, but he's building it atop a dirty empire.

Even so, the deplorable Gabriel Easton is trying to change.

For me.

Everyone has to start somewhere, I guess. Even the asshole who propositioned me in a prison parking lot.

"You have a lot of work ahead of you then," I whisper. "A lot of groveling. A lot of deep internal reflection. *A lot* of *everything.*"

A smirk slowly spreads across his mouth. "I can't wait to

get you into our hotel room so I can ..." He leans in and teases my lips with the tip of his tongue, "... hold your hand all night."

I burst with laughter. "You'll be groping me within five minutes after takeoff."

"Probably." He grins, and it makes him look oddly boyish. "Ready?"

I sigh heavily. "Yup."

That's the precise moment that the plane explodes.

If you enjoyed Gabriel Fallen, please consider leaving a review

SNEAK PEEK - DIRTY EMPIRE

Mercy

I want to be better for you. I want to deserve you.

Gabriel said those words to me. He whispered them as he pressed his forehead against mine, and my heart fluttered at the thought that this reprehensible man I've somehow grown fond of could—would—change his criminal ways for *me*. In my mind, he was making me a promise. The kind you make when you're in love with another person and want to change.

And then the private jet we were about to climb into exploded into a fireball and the reality of who Gabriel is and the kind of life he leads came crashing down.

Now, sitting on Gabriel's couch hours after being surrounded by a circus of sirens, emergency workers, and city and state law enforcement, I can hear the blast of metal, feel the intense heat of the fireball, and smell the ash and black smoke as if I'm still at the airfield. But it's Gabriel's and Caleb's pained screams for their perished friends that fill center stage in my numbed mind.

"Mercy."

It takes me a moment to focus on Gabriel's handsome face. He's perched on the edge of the coffee table in front of me, his calloused hands woven through mine, a somber expression pulling his brow tight as he studies me. I recall the first time I encountered those stormy blue eyes at Fulcort Penitentiary. We were there to visit our fathers: mine, a kind, loving man wrongly convicted of murder; his, a hardened crime boss who should be serving twenty times the sentence handed down to him. Whatever Vlad Easton was sentenced to is a misdemeanor compared to what he's done in his lifetime.

I remember thinking Gabriel a wildly attractive man, with that chiseled jaw and plump lips and playboy swagger. But he was affiliated with a dangerous inmate and therefore someone I wanted to stay far away from. His indecent proposal a week later—that I stay with him in exchange for his providing protection for my father—only confirmed it.

And yet here I am.

"Are you all right?" Gabriel asks, his raspy voice unusually soft.

I nod absently, though the last thing I feel right now is all right.

"She needs something to take the edge off." Gabriel's brother, Caleb, hands him a tumbler glass of amber liquid. Gabriel wordlessly slips it into my grasp. It must be the scotch Caleb cracked as soon as we strolled through the front door. I only noticed because it's not his usual thirty-eight-thousand-dollar vodka. I thought it strange at the time that he bypassed his favorite. Funny, the things you notice when you're in shock.

I'd rather drink gasoline than scotch, but I tip my head

back and pour it down my throat anyway, relishing the burn of hard liquor, barely aware of the taste.

"That a girl," Gabriel croons, smoothing a hand over my bare knee.

"Ready for another?" Caleb tops his own glass.

I swallow and shake my head. Only then do I notice my best friend is missing. "Where did Michelle go?" There's a hint of panic in my voice. Did she change her mind and take off?

"I sent her up to my room to take a nice, hot shower," Caleb says, his tone dispassionate.

Normally I'd have some quip, some warning, some ring of an alarm inside my head at the idea of Michelle getting too close and comfortable with Gabriel's brother, a manwhore by anyone's standards. Now, all I can think about is how Michelle could have already boarded that plane with Caleb while she waited for me to arrive.

My best friend could have died tonight, simply for being connected to me.

We *all* could have died, if not for road construction that made Gabriel and me fifteen minutes late. Pylons and fresh asphalt literally saved our lives.

And in the aftermath of the explosion, while we sat on that tarmac as emergency vehicles raced up to deal with the fiery carnage, and we ducked away from view of countless news cameras that congregated outside the gates to capture the scintillating story, Michelle remained startlingly calm. She told the police who questioned us nothing beyond the surface truth—that she was joining her best friend for a weekend in Vegas to celebrate my having written my last college exam. She didn't so much as hint at the other, more vital details that she is *fully* aware of—that she was traveling with a well-known crime family and that every minute of the trip had likely been bought and paid for with drug money. She played clueless, beautiful arm candy to perfection.

When Gabriel instructed our driver to bring us home, Michelle didn't demand to be dropped off at her house, she didn't tell me to get the hell away from her. She clasped my hand and said she was going wherever I was going, even as her fingers shook.

I'll never find a friend like her again.

And tonight, I almost lost her.

But Gabriel and Caleb... they *did* lose people.

"I'm sorry about Felix and Finn," I offer, my voice sounding hollow to me. I didn't know either of them well, and can't say that I liked what I knew of them, but it was clear by Gabriel's and Caleb's horrified expressions after the explosion and their somber demeanor since that the twins were important to them. "And about your crew, too." The pilot and a flight attendant also died in the explosion. Four people, in total. All of them simply because they were connected to the Easton family. All collateral damage.

I'm connected to the Easton family.

How long before I become collateral damage too?

My stomach roils at the thought. "Who tried to kill us?"

"It was a fuel leak," Caleb says without missing a beat, dumping his glassful of scotch down his throat.

"That was *not* a fuel leak," I counter evenly. Does he take me for an idiot?

Gabriel's mouth twists. "No one's trying to—"

"Don't feed me the same bullshit you tried to feed the cops. They didn't buy it either." I saw the looks, the whispers of "Easton" on lips. Everyone there knew who Gabriel and Caleb are. It's virtually a guarantee that their investigation will conclude that plane was rigged with a bomb.

Unless, of course, Gabriel buys a more palatable report for insurance purposes and to avoid unwanted attention. I wouldn't put it past him—there doesn't seem to be *anything* they can't afford—but with the FBI rolling up in their black sedans, I doubt there's a price tag affixed to sweeping this one under the rug.

Gabriel's eyes flash to Caleb, where a warning glare awaits him. In the past few weeks, Gabriel has slowly begun disclosing details about his sordid life that I'm probably better off not knowing. He's hinted enough for me to know his family didn't come by their money honestly, that while the club he and Caleb own might be a legitimate a business, there's likely plenty running out of it that isn't. Hell, I've watched *Ozark*. They're probably laundering drug money through there.

But I won't get much out of Gabriel about tonight's attack while Caleb is here to toss out lies and guard his little brother's tongue.

"Why don't you go and take a shower? I'll join you soon." Gabriel squeezes my thigh.

Normally the promise of his expert hands on my body sends my hormones into overdrive. But I'm not ready to be dismissed so easily yet, not when my life is at stake here, too. "Do you have *any* ideas who did it?"

"Like Caleb said, it was an accident."

My anger flares. "What's wrong? Are there just too many people who want you both dead to keep track?" I imagine the list could be long.

"Come on." Gabriel stands and tugs my hands until I'm on my feet too.

"I don't feel like a shower—"

"For fuck's sake, would you listen for once?" His soft-spoken words from only moments ago have evaporated with impatience.

"Sure. After you stop lying to me!" We had an agreement that Gabriel wouldn't peddle false tales about his life and who he is. Mind you, we agreed to abide by a "don't ask, don't tell" rule. I guess I'm the first to break the agreement, because I'm asking.

A metal click sounds, pulling my attention to the bar. My body tenses at the sight of Caleb checking a handgun bullet chamber, his handsome face a mask of grim determination.

I'm sure there are plenty tucked away all over this mansion, at the ready just in case. While it's not the first gun I've seen–the handgun Dad made me buy for home protection when he went to prison is still wrapped in a shoebox and stuffed into the back of my cramped apartment closet–it's the first time I've seen either of these two brandishing them so openly. That's odd, now that I think about it, given who they are.

"My brother and I need to discuss a few things, and you can't be a part of that conversation. Why don't you go and take that shower. *Now.*" Caleb's voice is eerily calm.

Neither Easton man has ever given me any indication that they would physically hurt me if I didn't comply with their demands, but things are different. Dangerous. Maybe giving these guys attitude isn't the smartest move at the moment.

Gabriel's looming height and muscular frame suddenly make me feel small and powerless. "Come on. I'll be right behind you," he whispers. He leans in to press a kiss against my temple before coaxing me toward his private wing of the house with a firm hand pressed against the small of my back.

I steal another glance as Caleb pulls a second gun from somewhere below the counter. *I'll be right behind you, my ass.* My gut tells me these two will be conspiring over possible suspects and how to exact retribution—the kind that doesn't involve law enforcement and arrests—late into the night. I'm not sure how I feel about that, given their targets nearly killed me tonight.

I don't know how I feel about *anything* anymore.

Including Gabriel.

My legs are wobbly as I head for the bedroom, hoping a hot shower will help me shake this icy feeling that has seized my limbs.

Gabriel

I watch Mercy's slim, sexy frame disappear around the corner. With it goes all semblance of composure. "Who *the fuck* tried to kill us tonight?" I force out between gritted teeth. My fist grips Mercy's empty glass as I fight the overwhelming urge to launch it across the room and watch it shatter into a thousand shards. Adrenaline has been coursing through my veins double time for hours, ever since someone blew up our plane—and our two best friends, along with two innocent staff members.

Finn and Felix are gone. My gut spasms at the thought. It hasn't sunk in yet. I still half-expect to wake up Sunday morning to those two idiots strolling through our front door, looking for liquor to drink and women to screw. That's not going to happen though. Instead, their sweet mother is going to be receiving the most expensive floral arrangement we can buy ahead of us showing up on her porch with a blank check to pay for a double funeral.

There will be plenty of time to mourn them. Right now,

we need to figure out who put a hit out on us and when they're going to strike again once they learn they've failed.

"Take your pick." The muscle in Caleb's jaw tenses. He's simmering in that dark mood of his, the volatile one that is unpredictable, chilling, and can be downright deadly if provoked. I was relieved when Mercy finally left. He wouldn't lay a hand on her, but his words can be just as destructive, and she's already been through enough tonight. "We know the cartel didn't do this. Those fuckers would rather send our heads to Fulcort in a care package for Dad. So it's Uncle Peter or it's the Perris. Simple."

Our father's brother, who's been maneuvering to take over the entire Easton empire, or our family's sworn enemies.

"You *really* think Uncle Peter would blow up our plane like that?" Our own flesh and blood?

"After we dropped that picture of him in bed with the Feds into Dad's lap?" Caleb snorts. "We basically signed his death warrant. He probably sees it as tit for tat, and he's got nothing to lose, especially if he's guilty. Plus, we all know he likes to blow shit up."

And now that Dad's behind bars, if Uncle Peter takes us out, he and our rat cousins will control Harriet, Dad's code name for the lucrative family drug business. He definitely has motive for eliminating us from the equation, aside from old-fashioned retaliation—something he's always been fond of. "But has he even figured out we're onto him? Dad would have warned us if he'd put a hit out on Peter, wouldn't he?"

It's been almost a week since my last visit to Fulcort, when I informed Vladimir Easton that his own brother sold him out to the FBI in a power and money grab. It went over as well as to be expected. Dad turned heads with his barking and then stormed out, and we haven't heard from him since. Has he put feelers out to see if it's true and Peter betrayed him? Has he demanded Peter explain himself? Or has he decided the crumpled picture speaks for itself and dialed up his favorite reliable henchman, Bane, the one man he trusts to do his dirtiest work?

"That hateful old fuck wouldn't take too long to make his move. But, no, I can't see him putting Bane into play without warning us. You know, since we're his pride and joy and all that," Caleb mutters, his loathing for our father oozing through each syllable.

"So then how could he be behind tonight?"

"Maybe Peter caught wind of our arrangement with the Perris. We knew things were going to move fast once we set those wheels in motion." Caleb's gaze is locked on the night sky beyond the wall of glass in our living room. The view from atop Camelback Mountain of the Phoenix city lights below is the reason we bought this mansion in the first place. That and the privacy we're afforded all the way up here, to live however we want without prying eyes.

But now there are unseen enemies somewhere outside; watching, waiting for the next opportunity to take us out. Tonight was a close call. The closest we've ever had.

Caleb is right. The night we hatched the plan with Merrick and Vince Perri that would finally free us from our family businesses and a potential future behind bars, we knew there would be family members—including our own—who would retaliate if they caught wind.

But is that the case? If it is, how the hell would Peter have found out and so fast? Who talked? "Something doesn't add up."

Caleb tips his head back to polish off another tumblerful of Scotch. He reaches for the bottle.

"I need your brain working tonight."

He scowls but stalls short of pouring himself another drink, reaching instead for the pack of cigarettes. He lights up. It's a sign that he's rattled. He *never* lights up in the house. He doesn't even like it when others smoke around him. "Maybe Peter had nothing to do with this then. It's time we give our new friends a call and ask them a few pointed questions about explosives."

"I don't see the Perris for this." At least, not Merrick or Vince. Those two are like us. They want to get *out* of the family business, not in deeper. They're the one who came to us with answers about our mother's death that we've wanted for almost two decades: Camillo pulled the trigger on the gun, but it was their older brother Miles who brutally raped her beforehand.

"Camillo wouldn't think twice," Caleb croaks through an exhale. A coil of smoke sails from his lips. "If he or that psycho son of his found out about our little chat with Merrick and Vince, if they knew our end game? They'd make a move now to get rid of us once and for all."

Miles Perri, the oldest of Camillo's four sons, is indeed a murdering psychopath. Jury's still out on Leo.

"If Miles found out about our arrangement, he'll kill his brothers."

"That's why we need to touch base, stat." We haven't reached out to Merrick or Vince to tell them we won't be arriving in Vegas tonight. We wanted to wrap our heads around the situation first before we stepped out waving a "you missed us, you cocksuckers" flag in case it *is* the Perris behind this. For all we know, their oldest brother has them tied to chairs as he extracts information.

Caleb's phone chimes with a text. He promptly checks it.

"Farley?"

"Yup. All clear."

I sigh with relief. Empire is closed on Wednesdays, which made it easier for our security team to haul in the dogs to confirm that whoever tried to kill us tonight didn't also wire the three-story warehouse. It's one thing to blow up a small plane with a handful of people in it. It's pure madness to light up a packed nightclub. But we aren't sure yet who we're dealing with and it could very well be a madman. "We need to keep security detail on both the club and our home until we get figure it out. Is he on his way here?"

Caleb nods through another long drag. "Three guys will stay on this place, and three will come with us."

I have a feeling it's going to be a long night. "Who do we call first—Merrick and Vince or Dad?" Despite what we may think about our patriarch, he's done a few laps around the someone's-trying-to-kill-me block. He'll have solid advice.

Caleb scowls at me. "Dealing with Dad is not a fucking phone call, Gabe. This is an in-person conversation. A private one."

I groan. "Yeah. Okay." *Fuck.* Caleb and our father in a room together in the best circumstances is a terrible idea, which is why Caleb never visits him. My head's already hurting, thinking about witnessing this rare encounter. "I'll call Donny. He can make it happen." We've lined the Fulcort guard's pockets with enough cash over the years to earn us the occasional private meet outside of visiting hours. I feel sorry for the poor schmuck though. Vlad won't take kindly to being dragged out of his cell bed in the middle of the night. He's likely to sit up swinging. "Say we'll be there in two?"

"Three. Maybe four, if we have to shake a fed tail."

Caleb flicks his half-burnt cigarette into an empty tumbler. "We need to have a friendly little conversation with Uncle Peter and Vic first."

"Like, *go* there to see him?" It's my turn to stare at Caleb like he's the idiot. "If he's behind this, he'll be waiting for us."

"I hope so." He reaches below the counter and pulls out two more gun clips.

"Just a friendly conversation, huh?" I can't help but chuckle, though none of this is funny. With the mood Caleb's in, he's liable to shoot our cousin between the eyes without so much as a hello. And the sharp set of his jaw makes me think that's exactly what he's planning on doing. Those two have never gotten along, and Vic is a cockroach. The world could do without him.

But I can't help wonder how much worse will things get before sunrise.

Will we both even be around to see the sunrise?

"Farley and the guys will be here in ten and then we roll." Caleb nods toward my side of the house. "You want to give her a heads-up that we're leaving?"

"If I want to wake up with my balls attached, yeah." That woman has a sharp temper, and the Easton name doesn't seem to strike fear into her. I admire that about her.

Caleb eyes his wing of the house, where that cute blond is showering, and I already know where his head's going. Both heads.

Normally I'd warn him to keep his dick in his pants. Mercy has been adamant that my brother not add her best friend to his infinite parade of mindless lays. But after what happened tonight, everyone's on edge. I'm not about to cock-block him, not when he's this wound up. Maybe blowing his load in someone will clear his head enough to not start a war tonight.

Besides, Michelle has been eye-fucking him since the night they met. She practically dry-humped his lap the night he drove her home, if his version of events is accurate. That my brother didn't take advantage of that is a damn miracle.

"We hit the road in twenty," he announces with grim determination, marching for his wing.

I grin. "Thought you said ten."

"Your dick can thank me later."

Twenty minutes. Just enough time to make sure Mercy remembers me in case I don't come back.

Read Dirty Empire Now

ALSO BY K.A. TUCKER

The Wolf Hotel Series:

Tempt Me (#1)

Break Me (#2)

Teach Me (#3)

Surrender To Me (#4)

Empire Nightclub Series:

Sweet Mercy (#1)

Gabriel Fallen (#2)

Dirty Empire (#3)

Fallen Empire (#4)

For Contemporary Romance, Women's Fiction, and Romantic Suspense by K.A. Tucker, visit katuckerbooks.com

ABOUT THE AUTHOR

K.A. Tucker is the internationally bestselling author of the Ten Tiny Breaths and Burying Water series, He Will Be My Ruin, Until It Fades, Keep Her Safe, The Simple Wild, Be the Girl, and Say You Still Love Me. Her books have been featured in national publications including USA Today, Globe & Mail, Suspense Magazine, Publisher's Weekly, Oprah Mag, and First for Women. For more information, please visit katuckerbooks.com

Made in United States
Orlando, FL
04 May 2025

61021278R00127